I Am Forever

I0633668

Alex Baillie

chipmunkapublishing
the mental health publisher

Alex Baillie

Published by
Chipmunkapublishing
PO Box 6872
Brentwood
Essex CM13 1ZT
United Kingdom

http://www.chipmunkapublishing.com

Chipmunkapublishing gratefully acknowledge the support of Arts Council England.

2

About Author

Alex Baillie lives in Kelvindale in Glasgow. Currently, Alex works in the banking industry, he has been writing short stories since he was a teenager and he recently wrote a short screenplay that has been made into a film by the Royal Scottish Academy of Music and Drama. Alex's main literary influence is Philip K Dick, with novels such as "Time Out of Joint" and "The Man in the High Castle".

Other works that have inspired him include Philip Pullman's "His Dark Materials Trilogy" and "The Stand" by Stephen King. Alex aspires to write novels that challenge people's perceptions of normality and the nature of what reality is.

Prologue

As soon as he woke up Charles knew that something was wrong. He quickly sat up in his bed and surveyed the room, but as far as he could tell everything looked normal. Throwing off his covers he made his way over to the window and opened the curtains. It was still dark outside and the street was completely empty which wasn't unusual for this time of the morning. Charles was just about to close his curtains when out of the corner of his eye he saw a flash of purple light in the sky.

He turned quickly to see where the light had come from but struggled to see anything clearly. Charles rubbed his eyes, thinking that he was probably still half asleep and with that he closed the curtains and headed back towards his bed.

Suddenly he became aware of an odd sound. He cocked his head to the side, trying to work out where it was coming from. It was a deep murmuring noise that sounded like some kind of machinery and it seemed to be getting louder. Charles realised that it was coming from outside so he quickly moved back across the room and opened his window. As soon as he did he regretted it, the noise was becoming unbearably loud and Charles had his hand on his window ready to close it, when he saw a man sitting on a wall across from his house.

The man was looking directly at him and for a moment Charles thought he recognized him. He tried to shout to the man to ask him what was going on, but nothing could be heard above the noise that seemed to emanating from everywhere. The man across the street didn't seem to be bothered by it and after briefly staring at Charles he stood up and pointed to the sky. Charles looked up and again saw another purple flash, and with that the noise doubled in intensity.

Charles was thrown back into the room violently and he landed hard on his back. Winded and struggling for breath he felt the whole room shake under him, outside he could hear car alarms going off and roof tiles crashing into the street.

He pressed his hands against his ears desperately trying to keep the sound out. The whole house was shaking and his possessions were being smashed to pieces all around him.

Then, as suddenly as it started, everything became silent again.

Charles tried to regain his composure but his head was spinning. His vision was going in and out of focus and a moment later he lost consciousness.

It would be a number of years before Charles Freemore would remember the events of that night, and longer still before he would remember the man across the street.

I Am Forever

Part 1 - Changes

Chapter 1

Charles Freemore woke gently from his sleep. He'd been dreaming about the future again. He was straining desperately to cling on to the image, but it was already slipping away from him, and it wouldn't be long before he would have no memory of it at all.

Opening his eyes, he saw the sun shining through his bedroom window, and he knew immediately that he'd overslept. Checking the time on his watch he saw that he was due to be in a work in about twenty minutes, so he quickly got out of bed and threw on his dressing gown.

Charles was annoyed as he had set the alarm on his phone but for some reason it hadn't gone off. He looked around the room, but couldn't see it anywhere. He was sure he had put his phone next to the bed before he'd gone to sleep last night. After a few minutes of looking around he was still unable to find it, so he decided to stop his search and head downstairs to call his secretary using the house phone.

"Good morning Sir."
"Hi Lucy, listen my alarm didn't go off this morning, so I'm running a little late. Can you apologise and let Mr Reid know that I will be in as soon as possible?" Charles was annoyed, as this was an important deal, one he'd been working on for over two months now.
"Certainly Sir, will there be anything else?"

"No, that's everything. I'm going to have another scout around for my mobile; I've got some important info for the meeting on it so I'll head in as soon as I find it."

" … Ok Sir, see you when you get in." Lucy said after a pause.

Charles checked everywhere in the house but couldn't see his phone anywhere, so he headed outside to check his car just in case he'd left it inside.

When he got there he noticed that his hands free kit was missing too. Charles was now starting to think that someone might have stolen them. He checked to see if there were any signs that someone had broken in, but as far as he could see the car looked fine.

Just then Charles realised that he hadn't used his key to open up the car.

'Damn, I must have forgotten to lock it, when I got home last night' he thought.

He closed up the car and headed back inside to call the police. He was furious with himself for being so stupid, but he was equally as angry that someone had just helped themselves to his property.

Charles looked up the number for his local police station and then called them to explain that he wanted to report a theft. After a few moments he was put through to the appropriate department.

"Good morning, this is PC Croft speaking; I understand that you'd like to report a robbery?"

"Yes." Charles answered.

The Officer then gathered all the personal information he required, put Charles on hold for a moment and then came back on the line.

"Thank you sir" the officer said "now if you could let me know what has been stolen and when you believe this happened."

Charles began to explain what had been taken from him.

"My mobile and hands free kit were stolen from my car, and it must have been done during the night, because they were definitely there when I came home from work yesterday." As he said the words aloud, they suddenly felt hollow to him.

The officer paused for a moment.

"I'm sorry, mobile what?"

Charles couldn't reply, he knew the answer to the question was simple, but for some reason the words were eluding him. The more he tried to concentrate on it, the more distant it became in his mind.

"Sir, are you still there?"

"Yes, sorry, I'm just ..." He broke off mid sentence, trying to organise his thoughts. But it was gone now; all that was left was a horrible feeling that something wasn't right.

"Is everything ok Sir, I was simply looking for a description of the items that were stolen?" The officer asked with obvious confusion.

"Yes, I must apologise, I was mistaken. I don't think anything was taken from me."

"What about the mobile and hands free kit that you mentioned?"

Charles paused a second before answering.

"I'm afraid I've never heard of those, please accept my apologies for wasting your time, now I must go as I'm running late for work, my alarm clock didn't go off this morning, I suppose the battery must have run out." With that Charles hung up the phone.

Charles felt odd and was struggling to shake off the sensation. He went to his bathroom and splashed some water in his face to help him wake up. He sensed that the he had the beginning of a major headache coming on.

'Not enough sleep' he thought to himself and he made a mental note to check his Personal Health Monitor when he got back from work, he'd been putting it off recently and was at least two weeks overdue for a check up. He finished getting dressed and headed to his living room to pick up his keys. For a second his hand lingered next to the keys, but then he caught sight of the clock on his wall out of the corner of his eye and he hurried out of the house.

Charles worked in the heart of town at a brokerage firm, arranging loan deals for his already well-off clients to purchase land and property to make them (and him of course) even wealthier. Upon his arrival he greeted Mr Johnston and spun him a story about traffic problems being the reason for his tardiness. The meeting itself went well; their deal to buy a plot of land on the Southside was nearly complete.

Mr Johnston was planning to build a block of flats, which he would later sell off. The land itself was in an area already swarming with properties, and to be honest the last thing it needed was more overpriced and undersized flats, but the customer was always right, and this deal was going to make Charles about £5,000.00, maybe more.

Charles was still a little distracted by what had happened earlier, he was annoyed at himself for being so silly to call the police and was still confused as to why he had done it. After a couple of hours, he was bogged down in paperwork for the deal and was contemplating his plans for that evening. Some of the guys were heading out for a couple of beers, but it had been a long week so he decided that for once he'd just have a quiet night in the house.

When he eventually got home he was famished. As usual he'd worked through his lunch so he headed straight to the kitchen to grab a take away menu. As he opened the drawer to get the menu he saw an empty space at the right hand side of it. Instinctively he realised that something was missing, that something belonged in that space.

Suddenly, he remembered, it was his mobile phone charger that was kept there.
'How on earth could I have forgotten about my phone?' he thought.

Charles didn't get take away that night; instead he spent a frantic couple of hours desperately searching for his phone, but with no success. He was also trying to figure out why he had thought that mobile phones didn't exist. As he still couldn't find it anywhere he decided to drive into town to find a mobile phone shop and clear the matter up once and for all.

* * * *

Later that night, Charles was drinking in his living room whilst watching the television. He was trying to make sense of what was happening. When he was in town he had not seen one person using a mobile phone and the fact that every single mobile phone shop was no longer there had left him badly shaken. There was however another question roaming around his mind that was worrying him more.

What was a Personal Health Monitor?

Chapter 2

It was Saturday morning, so Charles normally stayed in bed until around 11am. He'd usually had a lot to drink on the Friday and never felt like getting up any earlier unless he had to.

His routine was always the same. He'd turn on the TV first and watch either the utter nonsense of people cooking pointless meals that no one in their wildest dreams could hope of recreating or he'd watch another repeat of Friends. Of Course, Friends always won and today was no different.

He dozed in and out of consciousness for the next hour. The always-perky Friends audience collapsed into a crescendo of laughter at something Chandler said and this jarred Charles awake once more so he reluctantly threw off his covers and got up.

He had a look outside the window, and was thinking about going for a run. However as usual, the sun was nowhere to be seen and it looked like it might start raining at any second, so he headed downstairs, made himself a very black coffee and put a couple of bits of bacon under the grill.

'A breakfast fit for a king.' He thought sarcastically.

Charles liked to keep his Saturday afternoons as free as possible, to prepare himself for his night out with the boys. His ex girlfriend Melissa had always been getting on at him to do stuff during the day. She always wanted him to experience a little culture, like going to an art exhibition or some such activity to expand his mind. He had really loved Melissa and always went along with her without too much complaint but he'd been working so hard this last year that they'd just drifted apart.

He had just about finished his coffee when he realised that he'd forgotten to let his mate Johnny know where to meet tonight. That was when he remembered about the phone. He had been hoping that this was some kind of joke or that he'd been dreaming, but as searched again for the mobile, he knew that it wasn't.

He couldn't deal with it right now. He decided he would do some exercise, that always helped him to focus. Charles stood about six feet tall and had dark brown hair, he was in reasonably good shape and had done a lot of running when he was younger, but recently he'd been spending so much time at work that he hadn't had any opportunities to workout.

He went into his hall cupboard to get his exercise bike, but it wasn't where he had left it. He shrugged it off and ran upstairs to get his stepper, which he always kept under his bed, but it wasn't there either.
'What the hell?' he thought. 'This can't be happening again.' He put it out of his mind and ran back downstairs and out to his garage. He had a treadmill in there, and there was no way that had been moved. He threw open his garage door, but again there was nothing there; save for his collection of unused tools and a bag of cement that had gone hard.

'What is going on here?' He thought as he walked into the middle of the garage and looked around.
"It was here." He said aloud. "Just yesterday it was here."

He checked the lock on the garage door, and it looked fine. He didn't understand what was going on, even if someone had stolen the treadmill, it would have taken a van and about four guys to lift it.

He went back into the house and picked up his phone ready to call the police again, but stopped halfway through dialling.
'What am I doing' he thought. 'I'm just going to get the same routine that I did yesterday, and what happens if I forget again?'

He decided he needed to speak to a friend, so he called his mate Mike Richards. He asked him just to listen for a second, and then explained about his exercise equipment and that all of it was gone.

"I just wanted to speak to someone else to make sure I'm not going mad here."
"Is this some kind of wind up Charles?" Mike said half laughing.
Charles stomach lurched, and all he could say was a muted "No."
"Well I don't understand what any of this is about. I mean, a stepper, that's what you called it?"
"Yeah, that's right." Charles answered.
"Well, I mean if you want to exercise using something like that don't you think you could just go for a walk, or if you really wanted to, just walk up and down your own stairs, I mean who would honestly want to pay for a step?" Mike said, letting out a little laugh.
"Mike man, it's not funny; I'm being serious here. What about the treadmill and the exercise bike? Those were really useful to me, they helped me stay fit, you've honestly never have heard of those, I thought you had an exercise bike at home?"
Mike paused for a moment.
"Ok, this treadmill that you've mentioned, why don't you just go for a run? It has to be cheaper than paying a

grand that you said this thing cost. I'll give you this, the exercise bike sounds like it might be useful, but sorry mate I've never seen one before, but even if I had, I don't think I'd want to pay a stupid amount of money for something that really isn't all that necessary, why not just go out on your actual bike? Get some fresh air, meet people that kind of thing you know?"

There was another pause and Charles wasn't sure what to say next. Then Mike broke the silence.
"Listen mate, I reckon you should make an appointment to see your doctor. You must have banged your head or something. Maybe a concussion, you know? Did you have one too many last night?"
"Yeah, you must be right. I might have done it whilst I was sleeping or something and just not realised, I'll speak to you later yeah."

In truth he didn't think anything of the sort, but as he didn't know what the hell to think, he decided that making an appointment with the doctor would be a good thing. However it was closed at the weekend.
'Of course it is.' He thought sarcastically.
'Because who could possible be ill on a Saturday.'

So he decided to go in first thing on Monday morning, and with any luck, nothing else would have vanished from his life by then.

He decided to do as Mike suggested and go out for a cycle. He made his way to his hall cupboard to get his old bike. He realised that he hadn't used it in months. Melissa had made him buy it, as she'd wanted to go cycling by the Lake. He had bought the bike, but he'd never made it to the Lake with her. Something had always come up, and in the end the idea was just lost.

I Am Forever

He thought about it some more, it was lovely up there; he thought that maybe he would take the bike up there and just spend a few hours exploring. Then Charles remembered that he was meeting his friends soon, so he decided that he would leave it for today and maybe go there next week.

He did however make it as far as the local park. Charles was surprised how busy it was. He'd thought that the place would have been practically empty as it really wasn't a very nice day. But on the contrary, the park was absolutely packed and everyone looked like they were having a pretty good time. Charles realised that it been literally years since he'd last been to this park, to any park for that matter.

After about half an hour of riding he got back to the house. He was out of breath and was clearly not in as good shape as he thought he'd been. He'd been using the exercise bike whenever he had the chance, but it was obviously no comparison to the real thing.

It had gone one O'clock and he was due to meet the boys for the football in about an hour, so he made his way upstairs and started to get ready.

He was just about to grab his shirt from the wardrobe when he spotted his laptop. He quickly went online.

Treadmill – No results found

No results found, Charles didn't remember that ever happening.

He tried again:

Stepper – No results found

Exercise Bike – No results found

Cross trainer – No results found

Charles quickly closed the lid of the laptop and took a step back. He was starting to get really freaked out by all this.
"What the hell is going on? Where is everything going?" He said, as he looked in the mirror and checked for bumps on his head. He didn't find any.

'I'm not crazy' he thought 'These things exist'. He made a promise to himself that he would speak to the doctor on Monday and he managed to convince himself that she would tell him that there was a reasonable explanation for everything.
"It can wait until then." He said, trying to reassure himself.

He grabbed his shirt and turned to the mirror as he buttoned it up. But he didn't want to look himself in the eye, so he quickly got dressed and headed back downstairs.

'Time to go' he thought. He was just going to forget about everything for the rest of the day, have a few drinks and a good time with his friends.

Chapter 3

The pub was about a five minute walk from Charles' house. It was an unremarkable place called "The Trout and Tickle" and it was the kind of bar that you find everywhere.

It followed the same format of looking slightly rustic, with a big fire place and a beer garden for the summer. It never played any music though; Charles had always thought that was odd. He knew most of the people in the pub and he always enjoyed the atmosphere, especially when there was a big game on like today. As he got to the doors he noticed that the pub seemed a little quieter than usual. Irene Doyle normally greeted him there; she was usually pretty drunk and often flirted outrageously with every single guy that came in, despite being happily married. However she didn't seem to be around today.
'Must be ill' Charles thought.

He went inside and made his way to the bar. Inside it definitely was a lot quieter, he normally had to fight his way through hoards of people to get served, but there was only a few other people standing at the bar today.

"Hello Charlie how's it going?" The barman asked as he approached.
"Yeah not bad mate how's you?"
"You know me Charlie, can't complain, now what can I get you to drink?"
"Just get me a pint of the usual Eddie"
"No problem. How's work been this week?"
'Quite shit' he thought to himself. 'Eddie must get bored of asking the same questions, every single day.'

"It's been alright, you know the usual nonsense" Charles said feigning a small laugh.

"There you are" Eddie said passing him the pint "That'll be £5.00."

"Did you say a fiver?" Charles asked incredulously.

"Yeah, what's the matter; it was the same price last week and the week before'

"Eddie, last week that same pint that you've just poured, cost me £2.30, what's happening here, inflation gone through the roof in the last few days?"

"Ah, you're pulling my leg Charlie. I used to enjoy it when the prices were that low too, but the bottom line is that ever since the quota came in, prices had to go up or I'd be out of business. Good try buddy."

Charles smiled weakly, got out a fiver and handed it over. He made his way over to the table that he and his mates usually sat at for the game and sipped at his pint. He didn't have the nerve to ask the barman what the hell the quota was all about. He looked around the bar and it hit him, no one here was drunk, no one was even slightly tipsy, everyone was quiet and there was a kind of strange lull to the place. The football had started but no one was cheering, shouting or anything. Everyone was either just chatting idly or staring blankly at the TV.

It was weird. The people in here were always singing and shouting but there was pretty much no chance of that happening today.

Charles finished his pint and went to the bar. He convinced himself that maybe he just needed a couple more drinks to get in the spirit of things.

"Back so soon Charlie" said Eddie, laughing. "You'd better pace yourself you've only got two to go after this one; you'll be done before the end of the game at this rate."

For a moment Charles wasn't sure what to say.

'So there's a four drink limit in this pub now, for God's sake. Well if that is the case, it's pretty ridiculous' he thought.
'Who doesn't enjoy a drink every now and then? What harm does that do?'

The barman passed him his drink.

'Another fiver' he thought. 'I'll be broke by the time I leave here.'

"Oh, Charlie, I meant to say to you, a man was in here looking for you earlier."
"Who was it?"
"That's the funny thing, he didn't give his name. He actually ran into the pub, came straight up to the bar and said 'Did I miss him, is he here?' I asked him who he was looking for but he didn't answer me at first."
"What did he want?"
"He was kind of angry and just stared at me for a second, I was about to ask him again when he shouted 'Charles, who else, bloody Charles Freemore.' I told him I hadn't seen you. Then he just looked at me for a minute. It was really creepy, I felt funny, I don't know how else to describe it. He just left me a little cold. That was it. He left after that. He just turned round and stormed out as quickly as he'd come in."
"Didn't you get his name?"
"Sorry Charlie, It was all over so quickly. I didn't get a chance to ask him."

'That's pretty weird' Charles thought.

Alex Baillie

"It actually wasn't long before you came in, you just missed him. Sounds like you had a lucky escape; I'd stay clear of him if I were you he looked like a bit of a lunatic."
"Yeah, sounds like good advice, thanks Eddie."

'What the hell was that all about?' Charles thought. He didn't think he knew anyone who would want to come looking for him like that.

Charles' mates didn't actually turn up, and so he watched the rest of the match on his own. He would have called them and kicked off about it, but truth be told the whole situation was starting to get to him and he didn't really want to deal with anyone else just now.

After another hour Charles got his forth pint from Eddie. Just as he thought, that was his limit. Eddie had reminded him of the rules on this and to top it all off Eddie also reminded him that he would actually had to leave the bar within ten minutes of finishing his last drink.

'It's become a bit of a regime this' he thought.
He started to question who would want to go and drink in a bar under these conditions; it wasn't exactly conducive to a fun and lively atmosphere.

Charles grabbed his coat and said a quick goodbye to Eddie and a few of the others in the pub. The whole thing felt so unnatural and he decided he just wanted to get back home as quickly as possible. The four drink rule in the pub didn't apply in his house so he would continue drinking there he decided.

On the way home Charles started to think that perhaps he needed to see a doctor right now, not wait till

Monday.   He hated doctors though, and he hated hospitals.   Despite how serious the situation appeared to be, he somehow convinced himself that it would all be ok and he continued home.

Chapter 4

After a couple of hours drinking alone in the house, Charles got bored. When he was fed up and a little drunk, there was usually only one place that he liked to go, and that was the casino.

He grabbed his coat and wallet and headed back out. The night was crisp and although he was walking briskly, he could feel the cold snapping at him. His inebriated state was allowing his mind to focus on the task a head. It was all a very welcome distraction to what had been a nightmare couple of days.

After a short walk he arrived at his destination. He looked up to see two bouncers guarding the entrance. Charles paused for a moment, composing his thoughts and steadying his speech, ready to answer any questions coherently and soberly. However as he was walked towards them, one of the men was already opening the door for him, and the other offered a convivial "evening sir", which Charles returned with a nod of his head.

The downstairs area had a bar at the back of the room. It normally served as a place to have a final nightcap before heading home. Charles, as he always did, ignored this and headed straight up stairs towards the main room. Although he didn't consider himself an addict, he definitely did miss the casino when he hadn't been in a while.

Charles, like most of the gamblers in the room, had a system. It was one that was surprisingly successful, and more often than not he would leave with more money than he started with. Essentially it was about being patient. He always bet conservatively, and as a result he was normally able to build up a sizeable pile of chips. His game of choice was blackjack, it was one of the most fast paced games in his opinion, but Charles felt his system worked best with it.

He didn't want to sit alone at the table, as that meant he would have to bet two hands on his own, which was very risky indeed in his opinion, so after walking around for a few minutes he sat at table with two other players. There was a young blonde who offered him a nervous smile as she played with her few remaining chips and an older gentleman dressed very smartly in a business suit who looked like he'd just come straight from the office. Neither player was doing particularly well Charles judged.

He put down a twenty and the dealer returned him ten two pound chips. The minimum bet was two pounds per hand, and that was what he always started with.

* * * *

After about two hours, Charles found himself about ninety pounds up. He was feeling very pleased that yet again his system had worked for him. He was modest and never boasted to the croupier or other players, but he always wondered why no one else adopted his simple approach.

He decided that he'd pushed his luck long enough on the blackjack table, so he threw the dealer a small tip, said goodbye to the his fellow players and headed towards the roulette table. He almost always lost at that game, but he would always give it one or two attempts, and see if the luck was on his side tonight. Predictably, when Charles had put ten pounds on black, the ball had fallen onto red and when he put five two pound chips on five different corners, the ball fell into zero.

He wasn't the only one having bad luck on the roulette table that night. He observed with some sadness a man who had put down a twenty pound bet spread over a few different numbers, but had won nothing, that same man had then gone to the cash machine and withdrawn another twenty pounds and gone straight back to the table. This unnamed and never to be known individual repeated this loop four more times, each time not winning a single thing.

'Addiction is a sad thing' Charles thought, and he didn't know what was fuelling this man's habit. Perhaps he was someone with nothing to lose, perhaps someone with everything to lose. Maybe there was no reason, maybe this man just needed to gamble and it wasn't any deeper than that. Charles was only grateful that he was able to walk away if it wasn't going well.

He decided to call it a day at the roulette table. So he picked up his chips and was about to go and cash up when he realised that he hadn't been the bathroom in a good number of hours. So he pocketed his winnings and headed to the toilet.

As he was washing up Charles thought he heard someone crying in one of the cubicles; he decided to check if everything was alright.

"Is everything ok in there mate?" Charles asked nervously.
For a moment there was no reply but then he heard the man clearing his throat.
"Yeah, everything's ok. I just had a bit of bad luck today."

"Well, don't let this place get you down. Tonight probably just wasn't your night."

There was no reply from the man after that. Charles wanted to say something else, but thought better of it. But then just as he'd half opened the door, he heard the man the say one final thing.

"I don't know if this will make any difference now. I'd like to think that I'm intelligent enough to realise that if I'm able to tell you, then it doesn't."
"What are talking about mate?" Charles said.
"If you can help it, don't kill his brother."

Charles let go of the door and went back over to the cubicle.

"What did you just say? Did you just ask me not to kill someone, someone's brother? What on Earth are you talking about?"

Charles was getting angry, he was just about to bang on the door and demand an explanation when he realised that it had become completely silent all around him. He ran to the door that led back to the casino and ran back though it.

Everyone was gone. Not just the people, but the casino was gone too. He was standing in an empty room; all he could see was the exit at the opposite side. He walked a few paces, his breathing quickening and his senses sharpening as he threw his head from side to side desperately searching for something familiar.

But it was all gone. He quickly made his way out to the street. He paused for a moment looking all around him, everything looked basically normal. There were the usual people having fights and shouting and screaming at each other across the streets. Some were singing whilst other people were hugging each other for some extra warmth. Everything was more or less how it should be.

'More or less, that's a joke' Charles thought sarcastically to himself.

But he couldn't bring himself to look behind him.

"The Chips I won!" Charles said aloud, as he quickly delved into his pocket.

All he found were his keys however, and so he hailed a taxi and headed back home.

Chapter 5

Charles had continued drinking late into the night. He spent hours watching television programmes that he usually despised just to try and take his mind off of what was happening to him. He stopped around midnight and slowly made his way to bed where he fell into a dreamless and very uneasy sleep.

The first feeling that came into Charles' head when he began wake up the next morning was one of dread. He always felt the same when he'd had too much to drink, and last night he had certainly pushed the boat out quite far. He lay awake for several minutes, mentally trying to prepare himself for the inevitable hangover feeling that was about to hit him. He stretched out his whole body and slowly opened his eyes.

He lay there for a moment waiting for it to wash over him, but he actually felt remarkably fine. He pushed off his covers and made his way to the wardrobe to get his dressing gown.
'Maybe I didn't have that much to drink after all' he thought. He quickly dismissed that thought however, as clearly remembered drinking a barrel load of beer last night, yet he felt as if he'd had six pints of fresh orange juice not alcohol.

Charles was feeling pleased with himself that he didn't have a hangover. He'd meet various people throughout his life who had claimed that they could drink as much as they wanted without ever feeling any ill effects and he'd always wondered how they managed it. The thought of all the beer bottles and food strewn across his living room floor soon dampened his mood though.

He decided to deal with them later and went to his bathroom to freshen up a little.

His mind wandered whilst he was in the shower. The events of the last couple of days started coming back to him.
'This is ridiculous. I must be losing my mind.' He thought to himself as he once again considered going to see a doctor. The truth was he was too afraid to go, that would mean verbalising everything that was happening and he thought it sounded crazy enough in his head. Charles was fairly sure he would be committed on the spot if he went.

He dried himself off, put on some clothes and headed downstairs. He lay down on the sofa and flicked on the TV.
'Columbo or Diagnosis Murder' he thought. Sunday television was always pretty dull in Charles' opinion and for a while he sat idly flicking from channel to channel. After a while he started to get an odd feeling like he'd forgotten something, so he got up and had a look around the room.

'Was I supposed to go somewhere?' He thought that maybe he'd promised his mum a phone call, but then he always promised that. After a few moments of looking Charles went to sit back down, it was then that he realised what it was. The living room was spotless. No bottles of beer, no crisp packets, in fact no mess at all.

He quickly ran through to the bin in his kitchen, but there were no beer bottles inside. He threw open his fridge, again nothing. The seven year old single malt in his cabinet was missing. Even his cheap bottle of vodka was nowhere to be seen.

I Am Forever

He continued checking the house, but couldn't find any alcohol anywhere. He thought for one moment that he might have literally drunk it all. But he felt fine, and he thought it was pretty unlikely that he'd polished off an entire bottle of whisky and vodka.

He was becoming frantic, and was starting to panic. He tried to get a hold of his emotions but the situation was becoming too much for him. He backed up against his kitchen wall and slumped to the floor.

He stayed there for about fifteen minutes, just staring out the window. A million thoughts racing through his head as he tried to grasp what was happening to him.

He got up, pulled on a pair of shoes and hurried out of the house and headed toward his local off-licence.
'There's one two streets away' he thought.

Almost immediately he broke into a run, racing to get there as fast as he could. To find proof that he wasn't going insane. After about a minute, he arrived and he stopped dead, breathing heavily as he stared straight ahead.

It wasn't there.

He didn't know what to do.
'I need to go the hospital, right now' he thought.
"So they can lock you up and throw away the key" he said aloud, shaking his head.

"Throw away the key. That doesn't sound too good."

Charles turned around to see his ex girlfriend walking towards him.

"Melissa. I didn't even hear you coming." He said trying to feign a smile.

"Are you ok Charlie, you're looking a bit upset?"

"Yeah, I'm ok. It's nothing really. I haven't been feeling too well in the past few days, that's all."

"Do you want to talk about it? Maybe we could get a coffee or a tea or something. It would be nice to catch up." She said with a smile.

"A stiff drink sounds good to me."

"What?" Melissa said cocking her head to the side and looking confused. Charles thought it was probably the same look that his friend had had when he'd been speaking to him yesterday.

He decided he had to tell her what was going on. She'd known him years, maybe she wouldn't think he was mad, but he didn't want to do it in the middle of the street.

"It doesn't matter. Ok a coffee sounds good."

They walked a little further down the street and went into their local Costa coffee. Charles thought every Costa was a local one given the sheer number of them dotted around. He ordered a black coffee and sat down with Melissa.

He thought she was looking really beautiful today. Seeing her again, all the reasons they'd broken up seemed so trivial. He thought that maybe they would have had more of a chance if he'd worked less, or paid more attention to her. He put it out of his mind though; he couldn't deal with that just now.

"Melissa. What I'm about to say will probably sounds nuts, but just hear me out."

"Okay Charlie, what's wrong?" She was clearing trying not to look too concerned but Charles was looking the worst she'd ever seen him.

"Okay" he said trying to force a smile "have you ever heard of a mobile phone?"

Melissa moved back in her chair and Charles could tell immediately from her expression that she hadn't. She was about to answer when Charles cut in again.

"What about a treadmill, a stepper or dumbbells?"

She shook her head.

"Have you ever heard of Alcohol?" he asked, this time waiting for her reply.

"Alcohol, she repeated? No what's that?'

"It's a type of drink" he said with a sigh.

"Sorry Charlie, I haven't heard of these things, are they some kind of new business perks you're getting?" she said with a smile.

He tried to smile back

"No Melissa, I wish it was that simple. Up until a few days ago, these were everyday items. I don't know why, but they've disappeared. They don't exist anymore, and I'm the only person that remembers them." He stopped for a moment, he didn't want to get agitated and scare her.

"I'm sorry." He said.

"It's okay Charlie, but I don't understand what you're saying."

"Mobile phones were, no they are, a type of portable telephone that absolutely everyone owns. Treadmills and what not, it's exercise equipment; it helps you to keep fit. Alcohol, it's a recreational drink. It's a bit like a drug. Just about everyone drinks it. You lose yourself for a while, you have a good time, and you feel intoxicated, drunk, whatever." He looked at her and could see that she didn't have a clue what he was talking about.

"Charlie, that sounds really bad. Why would you want to drink something that alters your senses or intoxicates you? I don't know about the exercise equipment you're describing, if I want exercise, I go for a run or for a swim."
Charles felt like he was having déjà vu.

"As for mobile telephones, what's the point? Everyone has their Personal Health Monitors, so even in an emergency if something happened to you, your PHM would alert the appropriate emergency services."
"Yeah, sorry I forgot about the Personal Health Monitor, I know that would help me if there was anything wrong."
He felt like an enormous weight was on him now and he didn't know how to get it off.

"That's right." She said, now looking quite bemused.

He got up from the table.
"Mel thanks for speaking with me. I'm really sorry again to have bothered you with all this. I'm going to see the doctor tomorrow. I need to go."

Before she had a chance to reply he'd headed out of the door. He paused at the end of the street. He knew he had to see someone to get help. He took a few steps back and was about to head to the hospital but he just couldn't do it. He again convinced himself that he would definitely go tomorrow and with that he hurried home.

Chapter 6

As Charles walked back to his house he suddenly remembered a time from years ago when he and Melissa were at Lake Moore. She had been nagging him for days about going to an international food market they had. Charles had wanted to spend the day in the pub watching football, like he did every other Saturday, but in the end he'd relented.

The day, for once, was perfect. There was hardly a cloud in the sky and Melissa was wearing a beautiful summer dress with a lovely white hat. Charles didn't know what to wear to these kinds of things, and so was wearing an awkward shirt with even more awkward shorts. Melissa re-assured him that he looked fine.

Before they went to the market they took a stroll to the edge of the lake. The view across the water was breathtaking. Charles watched some boats gliding effortlessly across the water and felt a little envious that he wasn't out there himself. He didn't know the first thing about sailing, but as a child he'd always been fascinated by it; his dad had promised to teach him, but he passed away when Charles was very young.

They went into a nearby shop and had a look around some of the outdoor clothing and walking shoes that they had. Charles could see the hills out of the window and thought how nice it would be to go walking there. He picked up a pair of nice shoes, but after a moment he replaced them and he and Melissa left the store.

The market was actually a lot of fun and as promised there was food from a lot of different countries. Melissa bought some spices, sauce and a number of exotic *items from all around the globe. She must have bought at least one thing from every stall there, Charles realised. Melissa would do just that though, just so nobody felt bad about being left out.*

After the shopping they walked down to the water and found a nice spot to have their lunch. Melissa had brought a big blanket with her. She threw it in-front of her to spread it out. The wind caught it almost immediately and blew it right up into the air. Charles jumped up to help her, but the wind was blowing the blanket out of his reach and it took him several attempts to finally catch the rug and put it back down. He quickly weighted it down at the corners and then both he and Melissa collapsed in a fit of laughter.

They sat chatting and nibbling on the food for hours, and they stayed there so long that the sun started to set behind the hills that lay beyond the lake. He realised then that he hadn't been here since he was a kid. He'd went almost every other week with his parents, he remembered pestering them all the time to come, but as he got older he'd lost interest.

'Isn't it lovely' Melissa said.
She was gazing at the hills, a delicious smile on her face. She kept closing her eyes.

'How do you know it's lovely if you don't even open your eyes honey?'

She smiled even wider, and opening her eyes again she turned and faced him.
'Because I can feel it, silly, can't you?'
'I guess so' he'd said.

I Am Forever

The truth was that he didn't. He thought that the whole scene was very pretty, but he definitely wasn't appreciating it the way that Melissa was. It really was a perfect day, yet he was still thinking about what he was going to be doing later that evening, always focussing on what was happening next and not just enjoying the moment. Charles didn't like being that way, he wished he could just relax and take life more slowly, but he wasn't sure how to.

Melissa knew how to take it easy, of that he was certain, as he watched her, lying back with her eyes closed, lost in a daydream.

A little while later the sun was beginning to fade, and so they packed up their things and made there way slowly back to the car.

On the way back a curious thing was happening. A man was having a heated argument with one of the stall owners. They couldn't hear what they were saying to each other, so they decided to move closer. One of the men was practically screaming and seemed to be getting more and more irate. They were still quite a bit away but they could hear some of things he was shouting now.

"Where is he?"

'Where is he? Who on earth is he looking for" Charles thought, as he looked around the crowd of people.

A number of people had heard all the shouting and were headed over the stall to see what was going on.

The man who was shouting at the stall owner saw everyone coming and backed away from the stall owner and quickly headed in the opposite direction. Charles tried to see where the man had gone, but there was now quite a crowd gathered around and he lost sight of him.

Melissa and Charles heard the man explaining what had just happened to the crowd.

"He just kept shouting 'where is he, where is he'. 'Who are you looking for?' I asked. You should have seen the look in his eyes when I asked that, he looked like he was about to hit me, it was just pure rage."

"Who was he, did you know him?" Someone from the crowd asked.

"I've never seen him my life, but he told me his name was Green. He said 'Green, my name is Green; you should all know me by now! Now tell me where he is!' What does that mean?"

After a while the man got back to his stall and began packing up, and so Charles and Melissa resumed their journey back to the car. As odd as the incident had been, it hadn't spoiled the day, Charles had to admit he'd had a lovely time, but he was already making his excuses to Melissa about having to hurry back as he was meeting the boys in town later. She smiled a less honest smile this time. He knew she was unhappy and that he really should spend the evening with her, but he didn't.

Chapter 7

Charles woke at around six o'clock the next morning. He opened his curtains to see that it was a beautiful morning. The sun was just beginning to rise and everything looked very peaceful and quiet.

He sat back down on his bed considering whether he should go downstairs or try to go back to sleep. He scanned the room for a few minutes to make sure that everything was still there. Charles couldn't see anything missing, but he still didn't feel like going down stairs yet.

He would have to phone his work to let them know that he was going to the doctors, but what the hell was he going to tell them?
'Just say you've got a stomach bug, that's what everyone always says.' He thought, wishing that was all he had.

He lay there in bed for about another half and hour, barely moving and trying desperately to fall back asleep. He finally got up at around seven and started getting dressed. He was thinking about what he was going to tell the doctor later, but every version that he ran over in his mind sounded insane.

He made himself some tea and sat down to watch the morning news. Charles normally liked to avoid the news, he was fully aware of what a bad place the world was and didn't need reminded of it every two minutes on the television. The main headline seemed to be something to do with NASA and under any other circumstances Charles would have been interested as he had always been fascinated by space but today he couldn't give it his full attention, so he turned it off and went outside to his garden.

It really was a lovely day, and as it was warm too, Charles sat drinking his tea on his back step. He never bothered to buy any garden furniture as he had always thought it would be a waste of money. He hadn't really considered it before, but even thought it was quite a small thing, sitting in his back garden was nice. He felt calm and more natural.

A while later, Charles checked his watch to see what time it was. It had just gone eight thirty.
'Right, time to call the doctor' and with that he dialled his local surgery.

"Good morning, Garber surgery."

"Yes, hi this is Mr Freemore, I need to make an emergency appointment with Doctor Allen."

"Certainly sir, I'll just check if she has a slot free this morning. Hold please."

'Oh God, why can't this bloody electro pan pipe hold music vanish' Charles thought sarcastically.

A moment later the lady came back on the line.

"Thanks for holding Mr Freemore. Doctor Allen can see you at Ten O'clock, will that be suitable?"

"Yes that sounds fine, thank you very much."

As he had a little while before his appointment, Charles decided he would go out for a run, thinking that a bit of fresh air might do him so good.

I Am Forever

Charles did a few stretches outside before he started to run. As he looked around again he noticed that it was the nicest morning he'd seen in long time. Everything looked so clear and the sun was starting to beam down now.

He set off and lost himself in the run; just letting his body go into autopilot for a while. He had to admit that he was actually feeling a little better. He was still very freaked out by everything that was happening, but he was hoping the doctor would be able to help. As much as he hated doctors and hospitals, he did trust them.

He'd been running for about forty minutes when he arrived back at the house, and he started doing a few warm down exercises and a few more stretches. He'd learned the hard way that if you didn't do this that your body was going to be in considerable pain for a good number of days.

He was just about to go back inside when his eyes were drawn to the side of his house. His garage was gone. His slightly improved mood immediately vanished and was replaced by the growing feeling of despair that had been washing over him over the last few days.
'Why is my garage gone, this is ridiculous...' wait he thought. My car was in there' but the car was nowhere to be seen. He swivelled around and looked at all his neighbour's houses. Sure enough not one of them now had a garage. More than that though, there was not a single car in the street.

Charles couldn't quite believe that he hadn't notice until now. Cars were something that he took for granted; he never considered to check for them not being there.

'That's why it's so quiet, and why I thought it smelled fresher today' he thought.

"Why is this happening?" he said aloud. He noticed one of his less subtle nosey neighbours looking out their window at him.

'I just don't get it. Is this a sign or something, am I dying, what the hell is happening to me?' He tried to compose his thoughts and took a few deep breathes in.

He went into his house, quickly got changed out of his running clothes and headed back outside.

The surgery was only about ten minutes walk away, and as Charles appeared to have no choice but to walk, so he set off on foot. As he made his way onto the main high street that his Doctors were on, he noticed that the roads weren't completely empty. There weren't any cars anywhere, but there did appear to be several large vehicles of some description. He was curious as to what these things were, so he decided to get a better look at one.

As he got closer he noticed it appeared to be some kind of enormous tram. It wasn't like the trams he remembered from his youth, for a start it was about five times bigger. He wasn't sure, but he thought they were electrically powered.

Charles touched the side of the large vehicle. He wanted to make sure in his own mind that it was real. It felt cold.

He moved away from it and resumed his walk to the surgery

Chapter 8

He arrived at the surgery just before ten; the whole place was very small, Charles had always felt very claustrophobic here. In his opinion the numerous trips to see the family doctor as a child had only ever resulted in him being prodded, poked, or worse stabbed with a very large needle for an injection.

He was flicking through some of the awful magazines the surgery had. All of them were about three years old at least. It didn't matter, as he wasn't really reading them anyway. His mind was racing, he kept thinking that he didn't want to be here, but he didn't have any choice, he had to speak to someone.

The thought occurred to him that he should just be checking himself into the nearest asylum, but he convinced himself that the doctor would be able to help.

After a couple of minutes his name was called. He turned around to see the Doctor standing in the doorway holding her clipboard. He slowly got to his feet and walked towards her.

"Hello Mr Freemore, it's just this way." She said cheerily, and showed him which direction to go in.

Despite himself, Charles couldn't help but notice how beautiful she was. She was about the same height as him and had a very athletic looking figure.

She ushered him into the office and motioned for him to sit in the chair opposite her own.

"Now Mr Freemore, it's been a quite a long time since I last saw you." she said maintaining a lovely smile "What seems to be the problem?"

Charles hesitated for a moment, he would have to try and pace this out correctly. He thought it would be pretty easy for this to go badly wrong.

"Well Doctor, in the last few days, I've noticed that certain things have gone missing, I don't know if I'm forgetting them, or if they never existed or what, but things are disappearing from life everyday and it is scaring the hell out of me."

The Doctor looked confused by this, but Charles pressed on.

"Doctor, the truth is I don't know if I'm losing my marbles, the whole situation is just driving me crazy".

"Well if you can ask that, then you're most likely not crazy." She said with a laugh, trying to put him at ease.

Charles returned it with a small chuckle of his own.

"Just talk me through it; we'll decide if you're mad at the end, sound like a deal?"
"Ok Doctor, fair enough. Like I said, things are disappearing from my life. But it's not just my life, it's as if they're vanishing from existence and I'm the only person who can remember them."

The Dr regarded Charles for a few moments, and then turned to her laptop and started to type.

"I'll need more details, but believe it or not, what you're describing isn't completely unheard of. The symptoms you've described, of things going missing, or vanishing as you put it; well I've heard of them before. Anyway, I'm just pulling down your latest readings from the PHM."

There's that term again. Charles suddenly felt uneasy, as if the Doctor was taking a peak into his soul or something.

"Ok Charles, it isn't any kind of head injury as far as I can see. You're actually in pretty good health overall."
"Well, you said you might know what was wrong, did anything show on my readings?"

The Doctor paused for a moment, as if thinking how best she could explain something.

"Not exactly, there is something slightly unusual with your readings but I thought your symptoms sounded similar to a conditional called "The Shift".

"The Shift, what's that?" Charles asked.

"It's a nickname that we've, Doctors and scientists I mean have given to the reaction. No, not a reaction, the affects of the Syncar probe. Studies show that about one in every ten thousand seems to develop complications because of it."

"What is the Syncar probe?" Charles asked.

The Doctor leaned back in her chair

"Are you being serious Mr Freemore?"

It was becoming constant now, Charles thought. Everything was changing, everything but him. The worst part was that anytime he asked about it, people looked at him like he was insane or just plain stupid.

"Doctor, my symptoms, I told you, things are vanishing. Cars are gone, there is a quota on drinking now, oh and that's right Drinking has gone too. But it's not just that, things are appearing too. Like this PHM that people keeping banging on about. Four days ago a PHM didn't exist. So I'm sorry Doctor, I really am, but please can you tell me what the Syncar Probe is, because I really need to start getting some answers."

"Alright" She said after a pause "The Syncar probe was the automated space probe sent by the Syncar race. They're planet is, or was I should say, about eight light years away, but they sent the probe using their wormhole technology".

Charles was stunned and for a second, he wasn't sure how to reply to that.

"Are there Aliens on Earth now, did I miss that one too?" he said, rather failing to keep the sarcasm out of his voice.

"No, of course not, the Syncars all died. Their probe was the only source of information we've got about them. Their planet was destroyed in a tragic accident. If we'd only had their wormhole technology ten years earlier, we could have saved some of them. That's all they really wanted, our help. They saw that our races were similar and they reached out."

"How can that be possible? How is any of this happening" Charles said desperately, as he lowered his head.

I Am Forever

"You really don't know do you. I thought it could have been The Shift; the symptoms are similar, what with your losing things, as you put it. But that's not right, I can see it in your PHM, your Lobias readings are far too high; I've never seen them so high."

"What does that mean; please tell me in English Doctor"

The Doctor laughed a little at that.

"Sorry Mr Freemore. It means that it's real, but I don't know how that can be ..."

Just then the Doctor shuddered, but very subtly. It was so slight and quick that had Charles not been looking right at her, he would have missed it.

"Doctor, you were saying?" Charles prompted.

"Yes, Mr Freemore, from your PHM readings I'm afraid the results are conclusive. You appear to be suffering from massive paranoid delusions. In my opinion you are a possible danger to yourself and others."

Charles stood up and slammed his fist on the table.
"What! You just told me it was real."

"Mr Freemore, sit down, I've already signalled the police. They are on their way and they'll take you directly to the institute. You'll receive all the help you need there."

"What! You are the crazy one, not me. I'm leaving; don't even think of trying to stop me".

With that Charles got up, but the Doctor matched him and was already on her feet and blocking his path out.

"Doctor, get out of my, I'm not kidding, I will move you out of my way if I need to."

The Doctor laughed, but this time there was something more sinister to it.

"You must know that as part of my job I've studied martial arts from my very first day at medial school. It's a mandatory requirement for all Doctors, so I've been doing it for a number of years now."

Charles didn't know if she was being serious or not, but he decided he would just have to go for it, as it was that or just be carted off to the loony bin without a fight. He raised his hand to move her out they way. But in a flash, she parried his hand to the side and then punched him hard in the stomach. He collapsed to his knees, badly winded. The Doctor Stepped back for a moment, sensing his chance, he tried to quickly dash past her. Again though, she was too quick, this time she stepped to the side and swept his legs away from him, and he landed heavily on his back.

She then flipped his body over so that he was lying on his front and pinned his arms behind his back. Charles struggled and tried to free himself, but she was just too strong.

"Mr Freemore, I'm sorry for having to do this, it's clear that you've got severe problems, but this is for your own good. I'm going to give you an anaesthetic now. You've shown that you will attempt an escape at the first possible opportunity, so I can't take the risk."

"Please, Don't!" Charles shouted.

But he could already feel the needle going in and then a few seconds later the office started to turn to black. He fought as hard as could to stay awake, but it was no use.

He was falling, and a moment later everything went black.

Part 2 – The Institute

Chapter 9

Charles was fidgeting in his chair and nervously biting his nails. He was in the "Conversation Room" of The Elsmere Institute where he had been incarcerated for the last eight days, since the incident with his doctor.

He'd been into the conversation room every single day since he had been there, each time meeting with a different doctor and each time being asked the exact same questions. Nobody here believed him, everyone thought he was insane and they had no problem with telling him so.

After about ten minutes of sitting on his own, a Doctor carrying a file entered the room. He placed the file on the desk and went over to the mirror on the wall, stopped and then began to speak.
"My name is Dr Green." As he said this he turned around, walked slowly to the table and offered Charles his hand. Charles shook it briefly.
"The file I have in front of me details everything that you have confirmed has gone missing from your life."
"They are missing from everyone's life, not just mine." Charles said cutting in.
"Of course, that is something you have already confirmed to us, my apologies Mr Freemore." Again the Doctor smiled. "Well, if I may I'd like to start with the mobile telephones."
"Ok, Charles said timidly."
"As I said I've read your file, and I think I understand their purpose. But I would like to hear it in your words, what did the mobile mean to you?"

I Am Forever

Charles let out an involuntary laugh

"Is something funny Charles?"
"I'm sorry doctor; it's just that it didn't mean anything to me. Well, that is to say it served a purpose and it was useful, but I wasn't emotionally attached to it or anything."

Unfazed the doctor continued

"Ok then, you said it served a purpose. Broadly speaking, what purpose did it serve for you?"

Charles considered this for a moment.

'Is he looking for me to tell him what a mobile phone actually did or something?' he thought.
"All I mean Charles, is what did you do with the phone; you specifically."
"Well obviously I made calls with it."
"Ok, so you would call people for conversation, yes?"
"Yes."
"Why not just use your phone in the house?"
"Well, I would use it if I were in the pub or outside somewhere, I would sometimes need to speak to people when I wasn't in my own home, surely you can understand that?"
"The pub" The Doctor Said and began checking through his file "Ah yes, this was one of the locations that you could purchase and drink alcohol. Again, if I may, why would you need to call somewhere from this type of establishment. In fact before you answer that, tell me do pubs have any kind of public telephone in them or nearby?"

Charles didn't understand what he was getting at with all this.

"Well yes they do, generally, but so what?"

"Well, this may seem like an obvious question Charles, but why not just use the public phone?"

"It was... It was more convenient I suppose, I mean with public phones, they cost so much money ..."

"Cost money did you say? Sorry this is something that we haven't encountered yet. Charles all public telephones are free to use. They are run by a government organisation and do not even have a facility to accept money. So obviously this is a new entity which no longer exists for you, Fascinating".

The Doctor looked away from Charles and began furiously writing notes in his file.

Charles bowed his head. He thought of saying something to the Doctor, but again he wasn't sure what to say to make sense of any of this.

"Charles, I would still like to get to the route of what this phone meant to you. Apart from what circumstances you used it in, what else did you use it for?"

"I would send people text messages on it." Charles said quietly.

"Yes." Again the Doctor checked the file "This was sending brief passages of text to people who also had a mobile phone. What was the main purpose of this?"

Charles thought about it for a second

"Well, it was mainly just to chat to each other."

"Why wouldn't you call them, or better yet see them in person to chat. Sending a sentence in this way, seems, well a little impersonal wouldn't you agree?"

"It was just what people did, what they do! I can't be the only person who remembers all this. I know you think I'm crazy, but I'm not!"

I Am Forever

"Charles, I didn't say you were crazy. My only purpose here is to try and help you. You have my word on that, but to do that I have to understand and for that I need you to help me."

Charles lowered his head again. He had been stuck in this mental institution for the over a week and it was really starting to affect him. He couldn't quite put his finger on it, but something felt fundamentally wrong with the institute. More than that he felt lonely, he was cut off from everyone he knew. He missed them, Charles realised that he'd taken a lot of people for granted in his life and he made a promise to himself that if he was given another chance he'd spend more time with them and not be so consumed with his work. He missed just having a normal conversation where the person he was speaking to didn't look at him like he was something to be pitied.

"Doctor Green I'm not crazy. I don't know what is happening to me. I don't know what is happening to all of us. But it's bad, can't you see that?"

At this the Doctor sat back, and regarded Charles for a few moments and then got out of his seat.

"Charles, whatever it takes I am going to help you, I give you my word." He then began walking to the door.

Charles stood up.

"Where are you going? Is that it for today, Am I to go back to my room now, get doped up and then off to sleep until tomorrow where I get shipped back to this bloody conversation room to find out what else has vanished from existence!"

The Doctor signalled to the nurse outside and she opened the door. He paused and then turned to speak to Charles.

"As I said Charles I'm going to help you. This was just the first of many conversations that we will have. It will take time, but I promise that I'm going to find out what makes you tick."

Chapter 10

Charles felt absolutely horrible. He'd just had just been giving his morning dose of medication and presently was being ushered in the recreation room by one of the orderlies.

"Right down here Charlie, that's it. Those drugs sure hit you my man, don't they."

Charles couldn't speak, the words were somewhere within him, jumbled in his brain, but he didn't know how to put them in the right order, so nothing came out. His mind was still functioning relatively normally, he was fairly sure that he could still feel and think, but everything he did seemed so much slower.

He hated the way this place made him feel.
'That's the appropriate word, feel.' He thought drolly to himself. He couldn't feel much of anything right now and maybe that was the point of this place, to make you feel so inhuman that nothing really matters anymore and so you've no longer got any reason to be scared or angry.

The orderly, who was in his late thirties and must easily have stood at six foot four, was placing Charles in his seat. His name was Varity, and he was always smiling, never got angry with anyone no matter how angry someone was with him. Charles thought he was probably on more drugs than all the patients combined.

Varity patted him on the shoulder slowly, and gave Charles a big thumbs up accompanied by an even bigger smile. He tried to look back at Varity, but everything felt too hazy to see properly.

Then Charles was alone, he just sat in his chair gazing at nothing, unaware that he was slowly swaying back and forth. He was trying hard to be normal, but no matter how sane you were when you came into this place, it turned you crazy, one dose of medication at a time.

He slowly become aware of the happenings in the room, two of the other patients were playing a game of chess, except neither of them ever made a move. Charles had asked them about it a few days ago and Davy the older of the two players, had just smiled a sorry, sorry smile at him and said,

"Chess is a war Charlie, and you don't win a war by being hasty my boy."

Some other people were reading books, some talking, but the majority sat glued to the television. A soap opera was on and it had been on every time he had come to this room. Charles couldn't be sure but he honestly thought it was the same episode that was playing every single day, like some kind of awful twisted loop in time.

After about an hour of sitting in a catatonic state, his mental functions finally started returning to something like normal. He thought about getting up and possibly reading through one of the magazines. He was just about to do that when a fellow patient, Ian Clover, threw himself down next to Charles.

"All right Charlie, how's it hanging today?"
"Not bad Ian" Charles said managing a small chuckle.
Ian was from London, and had a wicked sense of humour. Charles still wasn't sure why he was here. He

had few tall tales and a notable amount of conspiracy theories, but so did a lot of other people in the world.

Charles always enjoyed hearing his wild ramblings; for a little while he could almost forget where he was. Looking at Ian he knew that he was about to receive another story just now.

"So what do you hear Ian?"
Ian sat back and smiled widely at Charles.
"This is a good one mate. Listen to this. There was talk of this baby being born a number of years ago."
"How long ago was it?" Charles asked.
"Don't know mate, let's say thirty five maybe thirty six years ago, give or take."
Charles nodded.
Ian continued with his tale.
"So this baby is born in Islington, and it's a normal baby, ten fingers, ten toes and everything seems normal. But here's the thing. It's a home birth because there was problems with the ambulances that night, and the Mum, she didn't have any money for the cab. So she has to do it in the house, give birth right there in her own living room."

Ian paused for a few moments, for dramatic effect.

"So you'd think that one of the neighbours, one of her friends or family would help her right?"

"Yeah, I guess." Charles said.
"No one did mate. I mean, she had family, and she had plenty of her friends in the street, but no one came. In fact, I hear that the entire street just looked out their windows at the house. They all heard her screaming, but no one came to help. So this Mum manages to somehow go through the whole childbirth on her own,

and she gives birth to a baby boy. Only, the thing is, she's lost a lot of blood and she's screaming for help, screaming the place down, but no one's coming."

"Why didn't she call anyone?" Charles asked.

"No one is sure, phone wasn't working most likely, or she couldn't get to it, don't know mate. Anyway, she's struggling and she's fighting to stay alive, but it's too much for her and she doesn't make it."

"She died?"

"Afraid so mate, she just couldn't hold on" Ian said gravely.

"What happened to the baby?"

Ian's eyes lit up again.

"This man walks into the street. The neighbours and everyone that's been pretending not to hear or see what's going on, they all shut their curtains and they all lock their doors because no one wants to look at him. This man, there's a shadow surrounding him, even if they had been looking they wouldn't have seen him properly."

"Why?" Charles asked.

"Cause he's not from here mate. This man, this thing, just walks right into the house. The baby, who's been crying its little lungs out the whole time, suddenly stops crying. There is complete silence. Then about a minute the later the man, walks back out and he's holding the baby in his arms."

"What he just took the kid?"

As Charles asked this, his eyes flicked up and he noticed that the CCTV camera was looking right at Ian and him.

'How long has that been looking at me?' He thought.

Ian saw it too, and put his finger to his mouth in the universal keep quiet motion.

"They're always listening Charlie, always watching."

The Camera was still on them, but Charles asked his question anyway.

"What happened to the baby Ian?"

"It was raised by that man, raised in the shadows. He's still around today, but heaven help you if you cross his path."

Charlie was just about to ask another question when Varity walked over. He put his hand out for Charlie to take and smiled his big smile again.

"Time for you to go Charlie, the Group is waiting for you."

Chapter 11

"He took them I tell you. He took them. Everyday I see him, he thinks I don't, but I see him. He sneaks up to my room, tip toes in when he thinks I'm asleep and he takes them."

A rather agitated patient called Derek Heath was banging on about someone stealing something and had been for the last couple of minutes. Charles was concentrating hard to try and work out what was being stolen and who exactly was supposed to be the culprit, but with no success so far.

"What is that has been taken Derek?" asked Doctor Bradley who was chairing the group today.
"You know, it's my stuff, all of it, he comes in when I'm asleep and he takes it, don't know where he takes it and I don't know why, but it's gone. He took all my money for the phones and everything."

Charles suddenly came to life.

"What did you say Derek?" Charles asked sitting up in his chair. As he did so the two orderlies who were standing with their backs to wall began to move forward, as if sensing a possible problem in the group. But with a shake of the Doctor's head, they moved back a little.
"Charles, it is not yet your turn to speak. Let Derek have his say, and we'll move on to you shortly, ok?" Doctor Bradley said in a gentle way, with a smile.

"Yeah, ok. Sorry, I just thought he said something about paying for phones that was all."

I Am Forever

The group laughed, there were six patients in total in the circle today, and they all seemed to find Charles' comment rather amusing. The only person who didn't laugh was Derek. He just seemed to be distracted and was muttering something quietly to himself.

"Now Derek, who do you think is stealing from you? Do you believe it is one of your fellow patients, do you think it's a doctor, someone else?"

Derek looked at Charles for the briefest of moments before looking back at the Doctor.
"You don't know do you?"

"I don't Derek, that's why I'm asking, I want to try and resolve this issue with you."

Derek slumped in his chair and looked at the floor.
"I don't know how to explain. That other doctor, he knows, I've seen it in his eyes when I talk to him. He is crazier than half of us if you ask me."

"Which other Doctor are you talking about? Do you think this person is the culprit?"
"They're always watching Doctor Bradley, always."
Derek said motioning to the CCTV cameras.
"I don't know who's taking my things, it isn't this Doctor, but he knows about it, I don't know how but he does. I've said all I want to say, pick on someone else today, I'm through."

"Doctor, may I speak now please?" Charles asked.

"Ok Charles, how do you feel today?"

"I feel ok. I don't like these drugs doctor; I don't feel myself when I take them. I feel disjointed and numb."

"They're for your benefit Charles. After your incident, it was deemed necessary for you to take this course for a minimum of four weeks. After that, if you are still showing improvement, we can look at reducing the dosage and begin looking into reintegration. Was there anything else on your mind today?"

'So many things' thought Charles, but he wasn't sure exactly where to begin. He was trying so hard to restrain himself so that he didn't look anymore crazy than they obviously thought he was.
"Yes, Doctor, Derek said something that I would like to ask about. He mentioned about money in relation to phones. I know this isn't necessary now, or that this has never been needed, but why did he mention it?"

"I didn't hear anything like that being mentioned Charles." the Doctor replied.

Charles tried to remain calm and forced a smile.
"Excuse me, sorry Doctor, but Derek just said it no more than a couple of minutes ago."

"I think you're mistaken Charles. But if you don't believe me, ask him yourself."

"Ok, thank you I would like to do that." Again Charles tried to maintain a smile. "Derek, I thought I heard you say a moment ago that someone had stolen your money that you were going to use for the phone. Did you say that?"

Derek looked at the Doctor quickly and then back at Charles.
"No, I'm sorry I did mention my phone, but not money, why would I?"

"Yes, why would you?" Charles said, failing to keep the sarcasm out of his voice "Why would he Doctor, what do you think the reason might be?"

"Let's move on Charles, what do you say? It doesn't do to dwell on the past like this."
"What do you mean, the past?" Charles asked quickly.

For the briefest of moments, Charles could swear that the Doctor suddenly looked worried, but he caught himself very quickly and again had his comforting smile.
"I mean that we've all heard your problems, but they're in your past now. You have to look to the future. One day you'll leave here and you need to be ready for the world. You need to be in the best frame of mind you can be in, and that means that you have to move on."

"Ok Doctor. I'm sorry, I will move on. I want to be a good person, and I will try to listen to all your advice and help. Thank you for helping and taking your time with me." Charles didn't mean it, but he had to try and get out of this place and if that meant playing ball and toeing the line then that would be what he would do.

Charles sat patiently listening for the next hour to everyone else's issues, some were minor, some were genuine problems, but he nodded along, showed empathy and was the perfect patient for the remainder of the session.

Despite the group being spread out in a large circle around the room, Charles noticed that the camera had been pointed at him for the entire duration of his one hour in the group. At the very end of the hour Charles looked directly at the camera. He was looking at it for about twenty or thirty seconds, all the while its gaze remained fully focused on Charles. Suddenly he saw

Derek trying to get his attention out of the corner of his eye. He looked over and Derek with a very worried look on his face whispered.

"Don't Charles."

Chapter 12

The drugs they were giving Charles made him feel inhuman and the dose he received before bed was the worst. Each night he would swallow the three different coloured pills he was handed and within minutes his world would quickly unravel. Colours and shapes would blur, he was seeing beyond what any normal person should see in their life. Gradually Charles' conscious mind would collapse into a stupor and after an undermined period of time he would wearily pass out. He didn't dream much in the institution, not that he could remember anyway.

Charles felt that his whole life had become some kind of awful dream. He'd been in the institute for a relatively short period of time, but the strain was becoming unbearable. Doctor Green seemed to be the only person there who was listening to him and the only person to date how hadn't openly called him a lunatic, in some respects Charles actually looked forward to his sessions.

Each conversation between them followed the same pattern. Charles would discuss his life and discuss everything that was disappearing and each day Doctor Green would tell him that one or more items no longer existed, or as he put it, had never existed.

Charles sometimes felt comforted that he was in the institute. He felt in a way that he was buffered from all the changes that were going on. Charles' biggest fear was that if and when he was finally released that he would no longer recognize the world around him. The thought of this made Charles feel more alone than he had ever felt in his entire life.

He continually thought about all the things that were missing and tried to rationalize whether he was being given some sign. Charles did not consider himself in any way religious but on more than one occasion recently he had prayed. Prayed for answers, prayed for understanding but most all he prayed for it all to stop. It didn't though, if anything the situation was getting worse. Each time Charles spoke with Doctor Green he felt more disconnected from the outside world, more and more things were disappearing and he was struggling to keep up with it all.

He heard the lock on his door click. They were coming for him again.
'Time for another conversation' he thought to himself 'Maybe I should just pretend I was making all this up. Would they believe me? Who knows, it's got to be a lot bloody better than this.'

Two men entered the room. They never talked to him. He knew to get up as they came in, as with or without his consent, he would be hauled out of there. Without any show of emotion they led him from the room and down the corridor to the conversation room.

Doctor Green was already inside. He was sitting at the table checking over his file, the file on Charles that he always had with him.

"Good morning Charles how are you today?" He said with a big smile.
Charles gave a non committal reply and sat himself down.
The Doctor nodded at the two people who'd accompanied Charles as they left the room.

I Am Forever

"Well, we've had quite a time haven't we? I don't mind telling you Charles that you are by far the most interesting patient I have ever had."

"What does that mean?" Charles said.

"Well, I mean all these things that you've made up, that keep going missing." and with this the Doctor laughed.

For a second Charles wasn't sure how to reply, he wondered if this was some kind of trick.

"What the hell does that mean? You can't say that too me, you're supposed to be helping me."

"Helping you? Yes of course that's my job, but don't get sentimental here, I couldn't care less about you. Your case is different and interesting to an extent, but the bottom line is that you're just as crazy as the others in here."

"Are you kidding me Doctor Green, is this yet another form of therapy to get me to react or something?"

"No, of course not, what do you mean by that Charles?"

Charles tried to suppress his incredulity as best he could.
"What do I mean?' he said sarcastically. "I mean that you are my Doctor and are supposed to help me and I was asking if what you were saying was a joke or a downright lie!"
"A lie did you say?"
"Yes, a lie, has hearing gone from this world now too? Will I have to speak up for all you to hear me now?"
"Charles, what is a lie? Is this something else that has gone? Great! Let me just write this down."

"You don't lie, is that what you're saying now? That lying has just ceased to exist?"

"Well as I don't know what it is Charles, perhaps you could explain this to me."

"Are you aware, or do have any idea what the truth is doctor?"

"No." The Doctor said in a very matter of fact way.

"It is the opposite of a lie. A lie is doing or saying something which isn't true which is make believe, not true in realty, something that is fake or fiction. Do you know what I mean?"

The Doctor stopped smiling at this and lay back in his seat for a moment.

"So people misleading others or not expressing their feelings accurately would be a lie?"

"Yes, that is roughly what I mean, but how can that not exist anymore. I mean lying isn't an object or a thing, it's a concept how can a concept vanish?

'I don't understand.' Charles thought.

"Charles, why would someone want to do something like this lying that you are describing, it sounds disgusting and horrible?"

Charles couldn't argue with that.

"It is wrong, but it exists and whether you like it or not people do it, I mean we wouldn't have any politicians without it, who would run the country without a few lies?"

"What is a politician Charles? The world is run by the quorum."

"They are people elected by the public to run the county, but they lie, they always lie."

"Charles that sounds awful, why on earth would you want someone like that ruling the world?"

"I wouldn't." Charles said "You're right; maybe this is one think that has vanished from existence which is actually good. I mean lying is rarely good and politicians never are."

The Doctor smiled at this and sat back. He then reached down into his pocket and pulled out a cigarette packet.

"Fancy one Charles?" The Doctor asked as he put a cigarette in his mouth.
"It really takes the edge off, you know?"

Charles put his head in hands and sighed.
"No I don't want a bloody cigarette Doctor, I don't smoke."

"What's a cigarette Charles?"

Charles looked up quickly and sure enough the Doctor didn't have anything in his mouth or in his hands anymore. And the smoke was gone from the room too.

This was the first time that something had vanished right in front of him. He made eye contact with the Doctor.

He was smiling again and looking straight at Charles. His hand moved to his mouth and looked like it was still holding a cigarette, but there was nothing there. He put his hand right up to his mouth and inhaled in as if he was still smoking. He held Charles gaze for the longest time and his smile got a little bigger as he blew the air back out of his mouth again.

"You know damn it, don't you!" Charles said shouting

"Nurse, open it up in here please." The Doctor got up and walked to the door. He paused in the doorway and turned to Charles.
"I know Charles, I've always known. I'm not who I said I was, but you'll be glad to hear that this is our last conversation, I have everything I need from you. I'm just missing one final piece of information now."

"And what exactly is it that you're trying to do Doctor, what has been the purpose of all this?"

"Why that's easy Charles, I'm trying to kill you."

Chapter 13

"Let me out of here! Let me out of hear right now!"

Charles had been banging on the door solidly for the last thirty minutes, ever since he'd been dragged out of the conversation room and thrown back into his own. He'd had more than enough of this place and now that Doctor Green had confirmed that he wasn't losing his mind, he decided that it was time to check out.

"Let me out of here, you know I'm not crazy now, let me out" He screamed again.

No one answered his cries. Charles listened at the door but no one was coming for him.

He slumped against the back of his cell and stared at the door.
'I'm going to rush the unfortunate person that decides to walk into this room' he thought.

Charles was rocking back and forth again when he noticed it. The institute was completely was silent. His mind flashed back to the casino when that had suddenly gone very silent. There were no footsteps and he knew that there normally guards, doctors and nurses continually pacing up and down the corridor. Charles couldn't hear any of the other patients either. The patients were always making noise, some of them talked to themselves and almost always very loudly, whilst others screamed or shouted.
'If it wasn't for all the drugs, I might have had some trouble sleeping with all that noise.' he thought sarcastically.

But this was worse, the silence. He felt completely alone for the first time since he'd been brought here. There didn't even seem to be any noise from outside, not even a slight breeze could be heard, everything was completely still and silent.

He got up again and went to the door. He was straining to see down the corridor, but it was very dark outside his room and so he could only see a little bit of the hallway. However the little that could see confirmed that there was no one there. It was hard to see because of the lack of light but Charles felt as if there was nothing beyond the little that he could see. He thought for a moment that that was a ridiculous idea but considering what had been happening to him, he realised it was entirely plausible that some of the building had disappeared.

Charles suddenly felt claustrophobic. He had to get out of that room, he was becoming afraid that he would be stuck in there permanently if there was no one there to come and unlock the door.

In his desperation, he tried to break down the door. He repeatedly threw his weight against it and kicked at it, but to no avail, it was just too strong.

He paced the cell for what must have been hours, his adrenaline not allowing him to sit down. Eventually fatigue did set in and he had to give in to it and lie down. He didn't want to fall asleep as he knew what that meant. Something else was going to go.
'What would it be this time?' he thought.

Suddenly Charles remembered an incident from a couple of years ago. He'd been in his bedroom when he'd heard a deafening noise. He couldn't remember the details and as he thought about it he began feeling incredibly dizzy. He sat up and tried to collect his thoughts and stay awake, but after a few more minutes he was struggling to keep his eyes open.

He tried to think back to that night, tried to work out what had happened to him.
'What was that noise?' he thought 'Why am I only remembering it now?'

Each time he tried to concentrate on the images and sounds though, he became more fatigued and finally it was too much for him. He passed out on the floor in what was the final remaining room left in the whole institution.

He slept so soundly that whole night. He didn't feel, hear, smell or have any indication of the dramatic changes that were occurring all around him.

If he had been awake to see it, he would have seen buildings and structures collapse and vanish all around him. What was happening was a complete reshaping of existence; nature had turned the tide of a battle that it had been losing for a very long time. New objects came into being too, strange designs and ideas that had never been conceived of previously, but were now free to flourish.

* * * *

Charles was awoken by the rising sun at around seven o'clock the next morning. He opened his eyes slowly but the brightness all around made him quickly close them again. After a few more seconds he tried again, he shielded his eyes with his hands and looked directly above him. The first thing he saw was a cloud in the sky.

He quickly got up and looked around him. The institute was gone, in fact there were no buildings whatsoever around and he was standing in the middle of a field which seemed to stretch for miles. He could see a forest ahead of him, but all the roads were gone and with the exception of himself there didn't seem to be anyone else here.

Charles stretched and let out a yawn. He decided that he would head towards the forest and just keep going in a straight line, to see if he could try and find some kind of civilisation.

He was about to head off, when he heard a noise in the field.

Someone was behind him.

Part 3 – Future Imperfect

Chapter 14

"Honey, what are you doing?"

Charles spun round to see Melissa standing in front of him and she was holding a basket full of apples.

Charles stepped forward and gave Melissa the biggest hug he had ever given anyone. He couldn't help himself, he had never been so happy to see someone in his entire life.

"Honey, are you ok? What on earth was that for?"

Charles slowly stepped back from Melissa and smiled at her.

"Nothing sorry, I've just had a bit of a rough time recently, but that doesn't matter now." Charles said, feeling a sense of calmness washing over him.

"Well Charlie, I've been looking all over for you. I thought I'd lost you completely for a while there. We've got to get the work finished soon if we're going to make it to River Water in time."

She then moved close to Charles again and kissed his lips gently.
"I didn't join with you my love, so that we could play about in a field all morning, so let's get moving young man." With this she let out a gentle laugh and held Charles hand.

Charles knew that he was married to Melissa now. In a way that he couldn't quite describe he actually remembered the ceremony. It wasn't like any wedding that he remembered but as he looked around him at how much the world had changed, it didn't seem so strange. There was virtual silence all about and the only noise that could be heard was the breeze gently ruffling the trees and the sound of bird song in the distance.

The institution had been in an industrial complex that was devoid of colour, devoid of life, but that had all been replaced by the most breathtaking scenery that stretched as far as the eye could see. Charles almost felt like he'd fallen into one of Monet's Wheat stacks paintings due to how sharp and colourful all the scenery was around him.

Melissa was still holding Charles' hand, leading him now into the woods that he had spotted when he first arrived. The trees weren't too dense and so there was a lot of light spilling through that gave the whole area a very enchanted feel. After around ten minutes of walking Charles saw a clearing up ahead and within that he saw a cottage.

"Is this my home, our home Melissa?"

Melissa cocked her head to the side and looked at Charles.
"Oh baby, did you bang you head or something? Of course this is our home, and we've got work to do this morning. I want to get the cows milked and the eggs collected before noon; I want to make it to the feast on time for a change."

"What is the feast?" Charles enquired.

"That would be the feast that the entire village attends." Melissa said very slowly, playfully mocking her husband. "Where we all meet each day, with the dances and the games, by the way, we might have to play football today; the Millers have been on at us to do it for weeks now? Now tell me Charlie, do you want to get the milk or the eggs today?"

'Well I have absolutely no idea how to milk a cow.' He thought. 'So picking up eggs it is.'

He found his way to the barn at the side of the cottage and cautiously made his way in. The chickens were rooming free inside, just going about there business without a care in the world. He began collecting the eggs into the basket that Melissa had given him, the job proved quite an easy one as they were basically just scattered at various points around the floor. After he'd been doing it for about twenty minutes he had to admit that whilst it certainly was hard work, he was enjoying himself. He felt a sense of satisfaction when he saw the basket full of eggs that he'd collected.

When he was finished he sat outside on a small wall, closed his eyes and for once, he just relaxed and let his mind wander. Since he'd arrived here, he'd hardly thought about his bizarre situation. This reality, whatever it was, seemed to be a naturally calming and beautiful place. The nightmare he'd been living in recently, no the hell, seemed to have been replaced by a little slice of heaven.

His mind raced back to the events of the previous night, and specifically to Doctor Green's revelation that he was going to kill him. Charles was confused by that statement because the Doctor had numerous opportunities to get to him whilst he'd been in the institute.   He tried to put it out of his mind and to concentrate on the here and now.

'That place is finished with, and so is he.'   Charles thought.   'Maybe you can't experience something truly good until you've experienced something really awful. Maybe that's the point of all this, that I needed to see how bad my life could be to appreciate what I have.' Charles thought this explanation felt a little hollow however; there were too many things that just didn't add up.   For now he was just going to go with the flow.   For even if he was only going to experience this world for one day, he was determined that he would enjoy it.

A little while later Melissa was finished with the milking and she joined him on the wall, shut her eyes and hung her head back a little whilst gently swinging her legs.

He stood for a moment, observing her, letting her radiance wash over him.   She was absolutely beautiful; he'd been a fool to let her go.
'Maybe this is a second chance and if it is then I'm not about to let her slip away again.'

"Hi Melissa, you awake?" He said jokingly.
"Hi you, yes I'm awake." She said opening her eyes.
"I'm going to take a quick shower before we go, ok?" And she got up and went inside.

'There is a shower in the house?' He asked himself. Charles looked all around him, and didn't see any power lines.   His house was a small cottage and up till now he didn't think it had anything other than a log fire inside, but then it occurred to him that he hadn't actually been inside yet.   So he made his way in and caught up to Melissa.

I Am Forever

"The shower Melissa, is it electric?"

"Electric?" She replied, looking at him slightly oddly. "Well of course it is it's not fire powered. Honestly you really must have had some kind of accident, do you want to go to the Doctors?"

'Doctors, well that's good, at least medicine hasn't disappeared.' However the thought of seeing another doctor didn't fill Charles with much confidence.

"No I'm fine honey, I mustn't be thinking right. I just didn't see any power lines, so I didn't know how we were getting our power."

"Charlie, are you playing a trick on me? You know perfectly well that we, like every other private house in the country get it through the sol power. You helped install it on the roof. Now if you don't mind, some of us have been working very hard this morning sweetie, so I'm off to the shower."

Everything here seemed like it had regressed, but Melissa had clamped that idea with the solar power, or Sol power as she called it.

'That's quite advanced and it doesn't kill the earth like most of the power sources I remember.'

He went into the bedroom and after a little searching found his wardrobe. He changed out of his dirty clothes and into a simple pair of trousers and a shirt. After a little more searching he found a pair of shoes to go with them.

He began looking around his new home and just like outside everything within was also perfect. There was a gorgeous log fire in his living room and a beautiful couch to the side of it. He saw that he also had an impressive collection of books which were held in a large case on one of the walls. Charles had always wanted to become more well read, but finding the time to do it had always been the difficult part, now that he thought about it he couldn't even remember the last book he'd read. He thought about how nice it would be to sit in front of that fire just relaxing, reading a book or cuddling Melissa.

As he finished looking around the house, he realised that it had everything that was necessary, without any of the useless clutter you normally find taking up space. He went back outside to sit in the sun on his quaint little stonewall and wait for Melissa. He almost fell asleep sitting there, basking in the heat of the beautiful day.

"Hi Charlie, I'm ready."
He opened his eyes and looked round at her. She was wearing the prettiest white dress, with a lovely blue floral pattern on it.
"You look absolutely beautiful Melissa. What did I do to deserve you?"

She skipped over to him and kissed him gently for the longest time.
"Ok Charlie, come on we'd better head off or we'll be late. I'd really like to get some art from Georgina Turner today, she paints the most beautiful landscapes don't you think?"

"Yeah, she sure does." Charles said thinking that it would be quite difficult to make these landscapes look anything but pretty.

Charles and Melissa then began making their way back through the trees towards to the town centre.

Neither of them noticed the man who had been hiding in the woods just past their house, who never once took his eyes off Charles.

Chapter 15

The town was about forty minutes walk from the house and Melissa was gently guiding Charles along. The sun was higher in the sky now and the light was scattering through the tops of the trees. Charles would have happily spent the whole day there, lost in the woods, exploring.

He asked a few questions, as subtly as he could manage about the feast whilst trying not to make it too obvious that he didn't have a clue about it. Melissa had explained that the gathering they were headed to was an enormous lunch and social gathering. Everyone who came brought some food with them and the idea was that basically everyone shared what was brought. Melissa and Charles were taking along some chicken and vegetables today.

Melissa was chatting about all the people they were going to see today and it seemed like an entire town's worth of people would be attending.

As they came to the edge of the wood, he caught his first glimpse of the town. There seemed to be some simple living accommodation and a few other buildings, which he couldn't readily identify. Near the end of the town, he saw what appeared to be a church, or at least a religious building. He couldn't be certain, but Charles had always thought that religious buildings looked a certain way.

"Is that the town church honey?"
"Of course Charlie that's the town's Church of Light."
"Church of Light?" He replied, hoping that she would elaborate.

"Yes honey, it is the place where we all go to help us worship the creator and the L*ight*."
Charles thought he understood the creator part, but he wasn't sure what the *Light* was?
"The L*ight*, what is that honey?"

She stopped smiling now, turned around looked Charles straight in the eye.

"The *Light* Charles, the *Light* is what made us. It illuminated our souls, when there was only darkness, for down that path led only Madness. The *Light* gives us hope, it fills our senses and with it we are truly blessed."

Then it was over, whatever had momentarily happened to Melissa was over and she was now smiling happily again, and began moving forward.

'What on earth was that about?' Charles thought. However, before he had time to dwell on it too much they had arrived at the town's centre.

In the middle of a massive courtyard were benches and tables, there must have been at least one hundred seats spread over the five enormous benches and most of them of them were full too. The majority of the people were deep in conversation, with everyone chatting about their respective work, trips they were planning and asking about each others families. There were at least fifteen people who were all attempting to chat to Charles and Melissa all at once.

Everyone placed the food on a sixth bench and once everything was in place everyone went to get their share for lunch, in what was essentially a large buffet. The whole group patiently waited their turn in the queue again continuing their conversations with each other.

I Am Forever

Standing there Charles chatted with Bob and Leticia about their kids and his fishing, to Laura and Dev about their farm and the trouble they'd had with drainage problems and to Ken and Louise about an upcoming composition being played in town tomorrow. Charles didn't think he'd ever met so many nice people in his entire life. More than that, he didn't think he'd met so many people at once in his entire life.

Charles thought if any burglars worked the area, it would rich pickings; there couldn't be a single person in their home just now.
'There probably wouldn't be any burglars here though.'
Which he obviously thought was a good thing.

That's when it hit him. The realisation had been coming to him slowly although he still didn't understand exactly what was going on, he thought he'd worked out at least a little of what was happening. He still had not a clue how it was happening, or more importantly perhaps who or what was making it happen.

But now the answer seemed so simple.

Life was getting better. All these things that were disappearing, he realised that the world didn't need any of them.
'People don't need phones or alcohol, don't need to smoke or drive cars, people didn't need to lie or be burdened by the hundreds of things that weigh people down in their day to day existence.'

Charles thought about how none of it was necessary, and actually most of it did more harm than good. Everything here seemed so much kinder and gentler. Everyone was happy; Charles thought about it and didn't think he'd seen a single argument over lunch.

Nobody seemed upset about anything. There wasn't anything to actually get worked up about he thought.

'Is this a mission from God, am I being given signs to try and help me, to help everyone?' Charles didn't think that he was a good person and in fact if he was being completely honest for a very long time now he'd been selfish and conceited. He'd been ruthless in his job and he'd pushed away the one person in his life that he'd loved, the one person that made him want to be more honest.

'What if this isn't a mission from God, what if it's just a second chance?' If that's what it was then he decided that he was going to take it. Even if he had gone mad, and Charles felt that was still a distinct possibility, then he was starting not to care.
'Because if insanity looked this beautiful, then quite frankly who cares what you call it.'

At the end of the feast, and after they'd chatted with at least a dozen more people, they finally made their way from the tables. A number of people were selling goods at the market and Charles and Melissa stopped by most of the stalls to have a look at them. Charles noticed a food stall and went over to have a look, leaving Melissa to check out the paintings she'd mentioned earlier.

He saw a few items that he wanted to buy, but realised that he wasn't exactly sure what the procedure was for buying things was here, so he politely excused himself from the stall worker and made his way back to Melissa.

He caught sight of her at the stall. She was holding aloft a painting she'd gotten, for him to see. He slowly made his way through the people and put his arm around

Melissa as she waited for her painting to be wrapped up.

The crowd that gathered round the stalls was so big that the Doctor managed to stand no more than ten feet from Charles without him noticing a thing.

Chapter 16

About three hours after they had arrived, the festivities finally came to a close and Charles was feeling exhausted. It was a mental tiredness rather than a physical one that he was feeling at the moment. He couldn't get over how many different people he'd talked with, and what he found most odd was the fact that every one of them seemed to be really good friends with both he and Melissa.

In the world before this one Charles had a relatively small group of friends that he saw regularly, but he rarely made new friends and he couldn't contemplate knowing, let alone befriending, this large a group.

It didn't feel wrong however, just something that he wasn't used to. Charles did have a feeling of belonging somewhere, and it was a feeling he hadn't had in a long time.

He and Melissa got their things together and they said a few final goodbyes before heading back to the cottage. Their journey home was at a much gentler pace than the journey in and for a while they walked in silence, holding hands and just enjoying the moment. Charles had always found it endearing that Melissa did not feel obliged to fill silence with needless conversation. So they walked on, at one with all that was around them and moving in time with the world instead of against it.

Charles was thinking back to the feast and at all the people there were.

"Melissa, how many people were there today?"

I Am Forever

She looked a little perplexed at the question. "What do you mean?"

"I mean it felt like almost everyone who lives within a hundred miles must have been there." Charles laughed at this, but that was certainly how it seemed to him.

"Well, not a hundred miles obviously, that would fall within Oscar del Piar village and the Lake Ranza Expanse." Melissa said in a very matter of fact way.

"So everyone from our village, our entire town basically, they were all there?'

"Yes of course. Where else would everyone be?"

"Well, how much does this cost to do this every day, how can everyone afford it?"

As he said it though, he instantly knew the truth. He didn't need Melissa to tell him what the answer was. There was no money here.

'No money' he thought 'it was the society people sometimes wished could happen, but there was never a way to do it.'

Charles thought that ultimately too many people needed their possessions and that deep down they didn't want to change their lifestyle. A utopian society aside from being a joke word was also a comedy concept to the majority of people.

'Everyone is and always will be greedy, perhaps not everyone though, certainly not Melissa. There are a lot of good people in the world but there seem to be an awful lot more bad ones.'

"I don't understand what you mean Charlie, everyone attends the feast, and everyone brings food and clothing and things they've made. There are trades of our goods and the village quotas for equal measurement are maintained, but ..." And with that she trailed off.

He caught her hand and smiled at her.

"I'm sorry honey; just forget about it, I was being silly."

They then continued their walk back to the house.

'I see that life can be better now.' Charles thought.
'I see it. I see that all these things weren't necessary. But what can I do about it? What am I supposed to do?'

For the first time since this nightmare began he was actually happy, happier than he'd been in years. Life was practically perfect here, as far as he could tell there wasn't one more thing that needed to disappear from this world. Everything seemed too good. He still wasn't sure what Melissa had meant by 'The *Light*' but he convinced himself that it was likely just to be a harmless religion and put it out of his mind.

They continued through the woods, a gentle breeze flowing behind them.

All the while the man in the shadows followed.

Chapter 17

"Dad is it much further?"

"No Charlie, we're only five minutes away now, are you looking forward to it?"

Charles shrugged and a made a funny face to show his indifference about the whole affair.

"I guess so." He said after a moment "But how long will it take, I mean do you get one in the first ten minutes or does it take longer?"

"How long will what take Charlie?" His dad asked him.

"To catch my fish Dad, I want to know how long it will be before I get my first one, what else?"

Charles' father let out a tremendous bellowing laugh and looked down at his little boy.

"What's so funny Dad?" Charles asked.

"Nothing Charlie, honestly, it's just that it could take five minutes, an hour or even three hours. The truth is Charlie that we may catch no fish at all today. Would you be ok with that, I mean do you understand?"

"Not really dad." Charles answered honestly.

"That's ok, you will my boy."

They kept on walking towards the pier and all the while Charles had a confused look on his face.

As they reached their destination, Charles looked up to see what looked like hundreds of seagulls circling loudly above him. He returned his gaze to the water and saw the waves crashing into the walls at the opposite side of the water from him. Across there he also saw what looked like twenty or thirty tiny ripples on the surface of the water.

"What are those funny ripples on the water over there Dad?"

"Ah, well spotted Charlie, those are the fish my boy, and if we're lucky we may catch a few."

"Great, well now we know where they are we'll be able to catch loads. Do you think they'll all fit in the car?"

Charles' father laughed again.

"Well see, but be warned just because we can see what we desire doesn't mean that we will necessarily get it. Now I'm going to get the rods set up, do you want to help me with the bait, if you remember how to do it that is?" He said with a smile.

"Of course I remember it is incredibly easy to do."

There was only one other person on the pier that morning. It was an elderly man who was sitting quietly in a chair, a little away from Charles and his father. He had a little black Labrador with him, and the little puppy with poking his head over the edge of the peer desperately wanting to see a fish. Charles waved hello to the man and the man smiled and waved back.

Charles was only eight years old, and was staring in fascination at his dad fixing the rod as he sorted out the last few parts of bait. The man in the shop had made such a fuss when his dad had bought him the little kid's fishing rod, so he was really excited about using it for the first time.

Charles decided that he wasn't going to have to wait all day, he'd catch his fish on the first attempt.

'And it is going to be a massive one' He thought to himself.

"Just you wait and see Dad, I'll catch us a fish big enough for us to all eat for tea tonight."

I Am Forever

His Dad ruffled his hair at this.
"Ok Charlie that sounds good to me, you all set?" and with this his Dad handed Charlie the rod.
"Now do you remember what I taught you?"
"I remember Dad, get the line to the side, then pick my spot and give it a good hard throw".

"That's right son, just don't let go of the rod eh?" He dad said with a chuckle.

Charlie looked at the water and after a moment or two he found a spot about half way across that he decided to aim for. He steadied himself and after letting the line sway in the breeze for a few moments he quickly threw the rod forward and cast the line deep into the water with all the strength he could muster.

"Good throw Charlie. Now leave it for just a moment, like we talked about and then gently, a little at a time start taking it back in."

"How will I know when I've got a fish on the line dad, I mean they're only little small things, will I even feel anything?"

"Believe me Charlie, you'll feel it, and you have to always be ready, you could get a bite at any moment and you don't want to be caught unawares."

Charles was slowly reeling in the line, a little at a time just as his Dad had suggested. The waves were strong today and on more than one occasion Charles thought that the pull he was feeling was a fish.

"You'll know when a fish is on that line my boy, trust me." His dad said seeing the look on Charles' face each time the line pulled a little.

Charles continued to bring the line back in and he was a little disappointed not to have caught anything on his first attempt. So he repeated the process over and over again. His Dad was now fishing along side him. Charles watched in awe at how far his dad cast his line, it was practically hitting the other side.

"You'll get there Charlie, don't worry." His Dad said with a smile.

They continued the pattern for another couple of hours. Neither had caught anything yet, but they were both having fun. Charles' dad announced that it was time for a spot of lunch. He brought out the picnic box and handed Charles his sandwiches and some juice too.

"So Charles." He said in between bites "Do you like it here?" Charles' father then swept his arm in a circular motion to illustrate the surroundings and scenery to his son.

"I guess so, yeah, it's nice here."

Charles looked out to the sea and saw a small island in the distance; he was just about to ask his dad if they could go there when he heard footsteps behind him. He turned around to see a tall man walking towards him and his dad.

"Edward, Edward I need to speak to you right now."

"Who's that Dad?" Charles said.
"No one, Charlie, can you just give me a minute ok, just finish your lunch, I'm going to quickly speak to that man, ok?"
"Ok Dad." Charles noticed that his Dad wasn't smiling anymore, he looked at the tall man and he was

regarding Charles with sinister smirk. Charles didn't like it, so turned away.

"What the hell are you doing here; I thought I told you the last time we spoke! You are fully award of what the rules are!" Charles could hear the anger in his Dad's voice. His Dad was trying to keep his voice low, but Charles still heard most of it.

"What's your problem Edward?" The man said it with such venom.
"You know the score here, but don't worry yourself, you won't see me again. I just wanted to pop in to paradise for a second. It's nice and warm here in paradise too isn't it, remind you of anywhere Eddie?" The Man then let out the most horrible laugh that Charles had ever heard in his entire life.

"Just leave Sam, before I do something I regret, you hear me, I'll do it."

"Oh, of that I've no doubt, we're two of a kind me and you Edward, three of kind if we count your boy there."

"I am nothing like you, you are nothing but a sub human monster, now leave!"
"Ok, Edward. Whatever you say, I'll be seeing you."

And that was it, the man walked away. Charles watched his Dad closely, he wanted to ask him what that was about. He wanted to know why that man so angry and how did he know Dad.

Charles' father, sensing these questions, came over and sat down next to him.

"Charles I'm sorry about that, I'm so sorry you had to see that. Just forget about that man, he's nothing, do you hear me Charlie, nothing?"

"Ok Dad, I love you Dad."

"I love you too Charlie."

Chapter 18

The next morning Charles woke to find that he was alone in his bed. Instantly his heart raced and a feeling of dread took over him. Sitting up in his bed he looked around the room but everything appeared to be normal to him. Charles wasn't sure if it was possible for people to disappear. Everyone at the institute had vanished, but he didn't know if there were really gone or perhaps had just gone somewhere else like him. The bottom line was that he still had no idea how any of this worked, and all that he was sure of was that he had no desire to lose Melissa.

Tentatively he got dressed and as he did he paced the room trying to find answers, hoping that he would have a flash of inspiration.

'A flash, I remember seeing a large flash in the sky.' He suddenly began remembering something that had happened to him a couple of years ago, but the details were fuzzy in his head. He knew that he'd seen something in the sky, but his mind was still having trouble visualising it properly. Then another memory started came back to him, and it was of a strange man who had been there.

'Who was that man?' Charles realised this was important 'Why am I only remembering this now?' He also realised that it wasn't just that he was recalling an old memory, it felt like he was accessing a repressed memory and his mind hadn't allowed him to fully access it until now. Charles was still trying to piece it all together when he heard footsteps downstairs.

"Charlie, are you planning to get up today, or do you intend to spend the entire day in bed?"

Melissa was alive, a great weight was lifted from his shoulders and he felt a renewed sense of purpose. He had remembered something important and his instinct was telling him that this was the key, if he could just work out what had happened that night he might be able to find the answers that he was desperately craving.

"I'm just coming now honey, sorry I must have overslept."

He put on his brown shoes, grabbed a jacket and headed downstairs. He knew where he had to go now and even though he wasn't sure exactly sure what he would do when he got there, he knew he had try.

Melissa was sitting at their kitchen table, sipping a cup of tea and reading a book. She smiled at Charles as he came into the room and then returned to her book. Charles poured himself a glass of water and after staring out of the window for a few moments, he turned to speak to Melissa.

"Honey, I want to take a little trip into town today, would you like to come with me."

"No problem, we're going to the feast anyway, where is it you want to go in town."

"I want to visit the church of light."

Melissa looked up from her book.

"Why do you want to go to that place Charles?"

"I have a feeling I may get some guidance there, it's just a hunch but I think that place is more than just a normal church."

"Well of course it is Charles, but are you ready for what it might tell you. We don't think you are yet, but ultimately the decision is yours."

"What did you say Melissa, who is we?"

"Sorry Charlie, what are you talking about? Anyway, yeah we can go the church of light today; we haven't been in about a week now so that would be nice."

'That wasn't Melissa talking to me.' Charles thought. 'For a just a moment someone was talking through her and they were trying to give me advice.' But the tone of what they'd said to him was bothering him, something about it seemed menacing. However he decided that whatever was happening to Melissa would have to wait for the moment, he was going to the church and was going to get some answers.

Later that day after the feast was over, Charles and Melissa headed into the heart of town and towards the church. It was impressive building that stood around seven storeys high. He realised now as he got closer to the building that it was a deep purple and blue colour, there were numerous windows on the building, but they had a metallic looking glass and he wasn't able to see through them. At the buildings front there was a solitary oak door just about double the size of an average sized man and to the right of the door there was a short message:

Through these doors lies illumination

'I hope so, I really do.' Charles thought.

"Are you ready Charles?" Melissa asked.
"I'm ready."

With that Melissa stepped to the right of the door, waved her right hand in a circular motion and a moment later the doors slowly parted and a hazy purple light poured out at them from within.

"Take my hand Charles, it's time to go."

He did as she asked and they stepped inside the church. Everything inside was filled with the purple light and it took a few moments for Charles to get his bearings to be able to see around. Eventually he became accustomed to it and he looked all around him at his surroundings. He immediately realised that it was like no church he had ever seen before. There were no chairs, no religious sculptures or paintings anywhere and nothing that he could properly identify as being of a religious nature.

To his right he was a large piece of machinery that was constantly contracting and expanding at a ferocious pace, Charles wasn't sure how but he knew that it was an engine of some kind. The metallic windows of outside were filtering down an odd gold light that was shimmering and merging with the purple hazes all around. At the far end of the room he was saw a screen next to what appeared to be some kind of electronic equipment.

"Melissa." He said pointed to the screen. "What is all that for at the end of the room."

"That is where you may, if you are very lucky Charles, speak to someone from the other side."

"Do you mean that machine lets me speak to the dead?"

"To an extent, but that is not its main purpose and that is not what you need it for, go to it now Charles, go before it is too late. He has nearly found you and you are running out of time."

Charles knew once again that he was no longer talking to Melissa, but he too realised that he didn't have long, so he made his way over to the other side of the room. As he crossed over, the sound of the machinery became louder and louder, it was a dull low mechanic sound and again memories of a couple of years ago flooded back to him. The machine in this room, he realised was what he had heard that night.

When he reached the display monitor he paused, unsure of what he was supposed to do next.
'How do I get this working, came someone help me?' He thought, and as he did, an image came on the screen.

It was a well built man, with blonde hair who seemed to be in his thirties. The man was sitting at a desk writing a letter and he looked very surprised to see Charles.

"Hello, can you hear me?" Charles asked.

"Charles, what are you doing in there, this is too dangerous."

"How do you know my name, and what is too dangerous, what is happening to me?"

"I'm sorry Charles, there's no time, he's going to get to you soon and I'm afraid it's not going to be pleasant, but if you've got any hope of remembering who you are then I'm afraid this is the only way."

"What does that mean, what have I done to deserve this?"

"I'm sorry, you have to go now, the link is breaking down, quite frankly I don't know how you managed to get enough power speak to me. Have you started to remember anything yet, anything that you can't explain?"

"Yes, but that's just it, I don't have an idea what any of this means."

The screen went blank, the link was gone. He felt Melissa's hand on his and he turned around to face her.

"I'm sorry you didn't find what you were looking for, but maybe we should just go back home now, what do you say?"

"Ok Melissa, take me home."

Chapter 19

Melissa and Charles sat on the porch watching the sunset. It was a beautiful night and they watched it go down with a glass of fruit juice.

"Where did you get this Juice Melissa? It is really lovely."
"D'Arcy Richardson traded it to us yesterday remember, we gave her those cabbages and onions. She makes the most beautiful Rastin in the entire county in my opinion."

Charles smiled and looked back at the sun setting over the hills. The drink was lovely, he had always been more of a fizzy juice person, but this was gentler, like everything else here.

"We'll have to get more vegetables over to D'Arcy so when get a couple more bottles of this I think."

"What do you want to get a couple more bottlers of?"

His heart sank, and slowly he turned around to look at Melissa. She wasn't holding a glass anymore and he realised that he wasn't either.

He'd only been living in this wonderful world for a short time, but he'd honestly hoped that he would be able to stay here, despite what he'd seen at the church.
'What was this optimism based on?' He thought sarcastically.
'Every single day things have been disappearing, and it's only been getting worse. Where is all this going?'

'It's was only a drink, I don't really need that.'

That was maybe the most troubling thing about it though. It was so insignificant, why would something like that vanish, Charles thought the world was surely only better with something like that.

"Charlie, will you build the fire, I think it might be a bit colder tonight. I fancy reading my book in front of it tonight, it's getting really exciting."

'So books still exist he thought, but for how long?'

"Sure honey. Do we have the wood here?"

"Yeah, but you'll need to chop it up. You don't mind do you?" She said with her best puppy dog eyes.

"I don't mind, I'll see you in a bit." He walked around to the back of the house and soon found an axe and the wood. He realised that he had never done anything like this in his life before, but how hard could it be?

He put the log on to the stump and raised his axe, carefully took aim and then swung it down hard. He had to laugh at the result; his axe was simply stuck in the wood, about half way down the log. He raised it again and smashed it down, this time the log separated into two. It was a very satisfying experience, though very tiring, he decided.

He stayed at it for another twenty minutes before realising that he'd cut way too much wood. He then gathered up as much as he could carry and went back into the house. He placed the wood on the fire and then realised that he wasn't sure how he would light it. He hunted in vein for a lighter or matches, or any thing that might ignite a fire.

Eventually, he decided to just ask Melissa, but to try and do it as subtly as possible so that she wouldn't think he was too much of an idiot.

"What do you mean you can't light the fire, are you playing a trick on me again?"
"Honestly, I've just forgotten, maybe still not feeling too well, anyway can you help or not?"

She looked him up and down with a smile.
"Ok, well you use the light bringer of course." With that she moved over to mantelpiece above the fireplace and picked up a small white object about the size of pack of cigarettes. She pointed it at the fire and tapped it twice. Instantly the fire burst to life, and the heat swept over the room.

"Wow that was amazing. I had no idea the technology here was so advanced."
"This little thing, this is just a child's toy. Don't you remember your history lessons from school; we acquired this in the technology share from the Drazen."

'Here we go again.' He thought.

"Who are the Drazen Melissa, are they from another village?"

In an instant Melissa turned. Her smile vanished and she looked him straight in the eye. Her eyes seemed to just glaze over.

"The Drazen came from the Siri star two hundred years ago. They shared their wisdom and fruits of their knowledge with us, as they saw what a peaceful and benevolent society we were. They said that they'd passed numerous other civilisations before finding

earth, but all of them were greedy, warring civilisations that did not deserve their friendship. Without them it would have taken us perhaps a thousand more years to reach the cultural and technological sophistication that our society now blossoms with. They are us and we are them, one species under God we now walk hand in hand across the stars.

"Do we have the ability to travel through space?"

"Yes, we have settled this solar system and a number of others. The Drazen taught us their wormhole technology which allowed us to travel almost instantly from Star to Star."

"But this world seems so primitive, I don't understand?"

"We know. This world embraces a simpler life, but that does not mean there is no technology. In this world, we live this life through choice because it is a blessed life. We travel the stars Charles."

Then a white light shone from Melissa's eyes and flowed into Charles and just for a moment, for a split second, he saw it all. He saw the travel between worlds that Melissa was talking about, he saw everything, just for moment.

"Help me. Tell me what to do, please."

"You are an anomaly Charles. We did not do this, there have been instances of time travel and dimension distortion in our past, but we are confident that this is not the cause. We do not know the reason for your travels, it may be the maker, it may be the darkness or it may the work of a species called the Driontin. We have

told you all we know. Please realise that your energy is very low Charles, darkness is coming to you soon."

And with that she switched, Melissa became herself again.

"Oh honey, I love this book, you should read it after me. It's an adventure story and I love the central character."

'What the hell was all that about. She keeps turning into another person and this other person seems to have at least some idea of what is going on. So in this reality, we've made contact with aliens and these ones still seem to be alive, or they've made contact with us he thought. There is so much I don't know, I need to try and piece this all together.'

"Melissa honey, I'm just going to get some fresh air. I'll be back in a second."

He walked over and gave her a peck on the cheek and headed for the door. What did that mean 'your energy is low' he thought? The whole thing was weird, and it was scaring him. He grabbed his jacket and opened the door.

There was a man standing in the doorway.

"Hello Charles." He said.

Charles was in shock, he tried to take step back.

"Doctor Green?" He said quickly.

The man just smiled, and then it happened.

Charles hardly felt a thing as the knife was plunged into him. He glanced down to see the blade sticking into his body; he couldn't really feel anything though. He looked back up to see Doctor Green, he was smiling and for the longest moment, they both stayed deadly still staring at each other.

"Why?" Charles asked.

He pulled the knife out and Charles slowly dropped to the floor. He was dying.

He lay on the floor looking at the doctor. Trying desperately in his final few moments of life to work out why, trying to figure out what it had all been for. The Doctor slowly faded away, and then the rest of the world bit by bit started to disappear.

A tree in the distance vanished and then another behind it. Soon afterward the house and everything next to it was gone, then the rocks, the sky and the stars. He saw Melissa for the briefest of moments and tried to say something, but then she disappeared too. Then everything was gone, and he was alone, the most alone he'd ever felt in his life. It was so black, black everywhere.

It seemed to stay that way for the longest time; all around him was nothing, just an empty void.

Then bit-by-bit a light started to appear all around him.

It quickly became the brightest light imaginable, and as quickly as the darkness had come, the light now filled up his entire world. He was in the light and he was part of the light, and suddenly he felt warm and safe. He started to regain some of his senses; it felt like he was somewhere now, in a room of some sort, he could feel again. Everything was still white everywhere, but he was now able to walk around. And then he heard the voice, a voice that he was sure he recognised.

"Hello Charles, I've been expecting you."

Chapter 20

"Hello Sam. Thank you for coming."
"Did I really have a choice?"
"Well, I suppose not, but I was raised with manners young man, so thank you all the same." The thing in the shadows let out a small chuckle as it said this.

It had a healthy disregard for most humans, but there was something about Sam that he found rather endearing.

"Where am I? How on earth did you bring me here?"
"You wouldn't understand where you are. As for how I brought you here, is that really important?"

Sam didn't say anything for a moment.

"Who are you?"
"I think by now you know who I am; a man of your intellect should have no problem solving that conundrum. Not to mention your little gift up there." With that, the thing in the shadows pointed at Sam's head.

"What is it about this guy, what is your is your problem with him?"

The thing in the shadows rushed forward and instantly a despair and horror flowed through Sam. Every part of him suddenly felt hollow and he just wanted to fall to the floor.

"You know what he is going to do, after everything I've shown you, after everything you've seen, don't play dumb with me Sam."

I Am Forever

"I'm sorry, please…"

The thing in the shadows moved back to its original position, pleased that it had managed to once again reduce Sam to quivering wreck, something it felt was no mean feat.

Sam composed himself.
"I'm sorry, I know what he is going to do, and I've seen what the world will become, but he seems so normal, he doesn't seem to be a bad person. I don't understand how he could be capable of it all."

"Let me tell you something Sam, I am not what you might call a good person. I've done some awful things in my time and I'll do a lot more. But no matter what I do, I'll never be him. He is an abomination who we need to wipe out from existence as soon as possible.

"You're so powerful; I don't understand why you need me."
"That's not how it works, I couldn't kill him if I tried, but you Sam, you're like him, and you're special. It has to be you. Just remember, if I hadn't saved you all those years ago, he'd have killed you by now. You've seen it with your own eyes, he tried numerous times, but I saved you didn't I?"

"Yes."

"Yes, I did. And now you're almost ready, but you have to believe, this won't work unless you have complete faith."
"I'm not losing my nerve ok. I just need to know more about him before I can kill him."
"I'll show you more if you need it Sam."

"Why did you choose me, there must be others that can do what I can do, so why me?"

"I chose you because you're a killer Sam, through and through. You're not an evil person; you just know what needs to be done. You can see what is happening to the world can't you?"

"I suppose I can, yes." Sam answered.

"It's choking. It's dying, and people like him, like Charles Freemore are walking among us, with their fingers on the button, ready to kill us all."

"I know."

"Good, then you know what needs to be done Sam Green. You're next entry is a hospital, you'll meet Charles there."

"Will I kill him there?"

"You don't know everything that you need to yet. You'll have to speak to him, probe his mind and learn from him. You need to learn how to kill him. So no, not yet Doctor Green, but you'll get your chance soon."

Chapter 21

Don't panic Charles, you're safe now.

The blinding white light was all around him. He felt like he was part of it. It was warm and beautiful. Charles felt like he was drifting on the sea. The whole place seemed to have a certain flow.
'But I'm dead.' He thought. 'What was the point of it all? Why did it happen to me? He just didn't think any of it made any sense.

"You're not feeling sorry for yourself, are you Charles?"

That voice again, Charles couldn't tell where it was coming from.

"Where are you, I can't see anything in all this light."
"I'm right here Charles, can't you see me yet?"

Charles looked all around him. It was just light everywhere, engulfing every part of him. He looked down and realised that he couldn't even see himself.
"What's happening? Where am I?"

The other voice laughed gently.
"So, you still can't remember, eh? Is the sound of my voice not even a little familiar, we spoke very recently you know. Well maybe you would prefer more familiar surroundings?"

Then in an instant Charles was in the middle of a field. But it wasn't just any field. It was his home with Melissa. He didn't know whether to be relieved or scared. He didn't give himself time to make that decision. He just started running, as fast as he could towards his home. He went on and on practically flying through the trees on his way back to the cottage.

He stopped.

The cottage was in front of him once more. He looked all around to see if the Doctor was still there, but Charles couldn't see him. In fact Charles knew he wasn't there. He didn't know how, but he could just feel it.
"Melissa!" He screamed. "Melissa, I'm ok, everything's ok now." He waited for a moment, just staring at the house. No one replied. Just then Charles saw something at the top of the cottage. It was smoke. Melissa must be inside he thought, and with that he started running again towards the door.

"Melissa!" Charles shouted again. He paused briefly at the door, for a moment he wasn't sure if he could go in. But he had to see her; she was probably the only person who would understand. He threw open the door and walked into the living room.

"Melissa ..." He said trailing off. She wasn't there, but a man was. He was sitting on the armchair, with his hands folded in front of him looking directly at Charles.

"So tell me Charles, are you ready to speak to me yet?"

Charles looked at the man for a moment. He had light blonde hair, cut short and was reasonably well built. It was the man he'd seen in the church he realised.
'This man has the answers.' Charles thought.

"Am I dead?"

I Am Forever

"You were stabbed through the heart Charles, not even you could survive that."

Charles sat down on the other chair and sank back. 'Why?' He thought again. 'What was the point?'

"We'll deal with why later Charles, but you have some more questions first, don't you?"

"How did you know what I was thinking?"
"I can sense your thoughts, Charles, but it is also quite obvious what you are thinking about, just by looking at you."

"Ok, where am I?"

"Well, you're home, in a manner of speaking. I don't mean this cottage, but to answer your next questions, this isn't heaven or hell."

"Have I been here before?"

The man leaned forward in his chair and smiled.
"Yes you have. You were born here, a long time ago."

"You said this wasn't heaven or hell, do those places exist?"

The man stopped smiling and lay back in his chair again.
"Yes. Not in any way that you are thinking of just now, but yes, they do."

"Why am I not in heaven just now, I was never a bad guy?"
"Do you want to be there Charles?" The man said, studying Charles closely.

"No." Charles said. "I want to be alive."

"Good! Heaven can wait, we'll get there eventually, or not. But for now we have some more vital matters to discuss. Walk with me."

They both stood up and instantly they were back in the middle of the field again.
"You have more questions Charles?"
Charles felt a little disorientated after their sudden jump to the field.

"Who are you?"
"I'm not God, that's for sure, so don't worry about that. I'm no other good or bad person that you'll have heard of, but you do know me. I can't fully explain to you what I am yet, you need to remember on your own, but I am not human. I have some abilities which very few of your kind have now."

"But didn't you say I was from here? What does that make me?"

"You're human, but you were born here. There is no contradiction. You left here when you were still a child; it wasn't long after your mother was killed."

"My dad said that my mum died giving birth to me."

"Your dad lied to you Charles. He took you from this place to protect you from some very bad people. You see, until I brought you back here, I was the last person to exist here in over a hundred of your years."

"Have you been on your own all this time?"

"Yes, but time works a little differently here, so you don't feel too sorry for me. I can leave, but I've had to stay to help you and to help fight the *darkness*."

"What is the *darkness*? I've heard of that term. The L*ight* too, I heard that before I died."

"Well, you've met two of them already, two of the people from the darkness that is."

"Doctor Green is one."

The man nodded.

"He's been after you a long time. He's like you, he has very similar abilities, but something happened to him when he was a child that has poisoned him forever. He is nothing short of pure hate now. As you've seen, he can be very charming and knowledgeable. He can blend in, and sometimes you'd never even notice him. But the bottom line is that he is very close to killing us all. I don't just mean Earth and your people, his influence could extend here and beyond."

"How could he, he's just a man, he's an evil man I know, but how could he do what you're saying?"

"Let's keep walking Charles." So they moved on together, in silence now until they reached the centre of the town.

"You have more questions, yes?"

"Why did this happen to me? All the things, ideas, people, that disappeared I mean did they even exist in the first place?"

"Yes, they did."

"Then why?"

"Well, let me ask you a question. Did you enjoy your life? Were you happy with how it was going?"

"Not really, it wasn't terrible, but I suppose there is no point in trying to lie, no I wasn't happy."

"And what about near the end of your life, was it better or worse?"

Charles was sure that it was better, of course it was better, there was no doubt about that, all the stuff that went away, most of it was so unnecessary. Possessions and power and the greed that wove them together were killing everyone.
"The whole world was choking to death. I get it, I really do. But that's how we developed. We weren't as peaceful as the people here" Charles said gesturing all around him."

"I know that when you arrived, you were a bit dazed, yes?"

"The light, is that what you mean?" Charles said suddenly. "Are you the light? I remember a rhyme."

The man interrupted him:

Follow the light that fights the darkness, for down that path lies only madness.

"I'm part of the light. That is just a name we were given by some humans, a long time ago. They were actually the first humans we encountered. They stumbled their way into this place, by a mixture of luck and recklessness. But we were impressed, very few species have ever made it here and we've tried to help you ever since. But this was before your species descended."

Suddenly the man looked worried.
"I thought we would have more time."
"What is it?"
"He's on his way, Doctor Green; he's coming for you right now. We need to get back to the cottage."

And with that they were there, standing by the fireplace again. Charles fought hard against the nauseous feeling.

"How is he here?"

"There is no time Charles. I'm sorry I didn't have longer with you. I'm going to help you remember who you really are. And I'm sorry Charles, I really am because when you remember, you'll remember what you need to do."

The man placed his hand gently on Charles' shoulder and said something, very quietly under his breath. Charles was just straining to hear what the words were when it hit him. It was a wave of knowledge and understanding that came over Charles so hard that he literally fell to the floor. The man fell back too; he collapsed into the armchair struggling for breath. Charles then heard a loud explosion outside.

"The Door Charles, Close the door!"

Charles looked at the door and it immediately flew shut.
"I remember. I remember so much. You're Di-Ar you helped me so long ago."

Di-Ar nodded gravely, and then he rose to his feet.

"Yes, I know, you remember now. But now that you do, you know what needs to be done. You have to start now. I'm sending you back. You need to go back and you need to start convincing people quickly, you know that you don't have much time. Find the others like you before he does."

"But there is still so much I need to ask you, there is still so much I need to know"

There was a pounding at the door now, getting increasingly louder. Di-ar looked up at it, worriedly.
"There's no time Charles, you have to go back right now, you just aren't strong enough to face him yet".

The man quickly grabbed Charles' shoulder again.

"Don't worry about me. I've lived a very long life; I've been protecting this place and you for so long now that I've forgotten how to do anything else. I had a wife and children once. The trust is Charles that I think it's time for me to be with them again. I will miss you old friend.

Another explosion rang out, and door flew off its hinges. Just then Doctor Green Strode into the room.

"Hello Charles, nice to see you again." Charles looked at his hands and saw that some kind of visible energy was pouring out of both of them.

Doctor Green then ran towards him.

"Go Back Charles. You have to leave!" Di-ar screamed.

"Now!"